"十三五"国家重点出版规划项目

白居易诗歌英译
Chü-e Pai's Poems in Chinese and English
With Annotations

赵彦春 译·注
Translated and Annotated by Yanchun Chao

上海大学出版社
·上海·

图书在版编目(CIP)数据

白居易诗歌英译/赵彦春译、注.—上海:上海大学出版社,2020.12(2021.9重印)
ISBN 978-7-5671-4064-6

Ⅰ.①白… Ⅱ.①赵… Ⅲ.①白居易(772-846)—唐诗—英语—文学翻译 Ⅳ.①I222.742②H315.9

中国版本图书馆 CIP 数据核字(2021)第 013800 号

策　　划　许家骏
责任编辑　王悦生
助理编辑　陆仕超
封面设计　王兆琪
技术编辑　金　鑫　钱宇坤

白居易诗歌英译

赵彦春　译·注
上海大学出版社出版发行
(上海市上大路 99 号　邮政编码 200444)
(http://www.shupress.cn) 发行热线 021-66135112
出版人　戴骏豪

*

南京展望文化发展有限公司排版
江苏凤凰数码印务有限公司印刷　各地新华书店经销
开本 710mm×1000mm　1/16　印张 21　字数 344 千字
2021 年 1 月第 1 版　2021 年 9 月第 2 次印刷
ISBN 978-7-5671-4064-6/I·623　定价 280.00 元

版权所有　侵权必究
如发现本书有印装质量问题请与印刷厂质量科联系
联系电话:025-57718474

序 言

亲爱的读者,也许你们知道,长久以来中国人都将自己的国家视为一个诗的国度,诗歌是人们最喜爱的艺术,也是人们最常阅读和吟诵的文学作品。作诗的才能甚至被视为一个人最重要的能力,在唐代(618—907)成为科举考试最热门的进士科最重要的衡量标准。科举试诗虽然在宋代以后一度废止,但到清乾隆二十二年(1757)又予恢复,这使诗歌写作成为应试之人必具的能力。由于古代封建社会的文化垄断和举世喜尚诗歌的风气,历代帝王、大臣和文武官员都能作诗。古代留下诗作最多的作者就是清高宗弘历,他一生写作了四万多首诗,数量接近唐代留下的全部诗作。历代自三公、宰辅至各级官员留下诗集者多得难以计数,这在世界范围内也是一个奇观。

你们即将要阅读的诗集,出自唐代中叶最为世人喜爱的天才诗人白居易(772—846)之手。这位诗人很早就显示出不凡的才华,五六岁就开始学习作诗,九岁已熟悉诗歌声韵。青年时代入京城长安应试,拿着自己的诗作去拜访前辈名诗人顾况(约730—806后)。顾况拿他的名字开玩笑说:"长安物价贵,居住很不容易啊!"可是当顾况打开诗卷,刚读完第一首《赋得古原草送别》,便连忙改口说:"能写出这样的诗,也就没什么不容易了。我刚才是开玩笑!"

因为得到诗坛的肯定,白居易在贞元十六年(800)27岁时考中进士。进士与明经是唐代科举两个主要的常设科目,进士以文学才能为主,明经以经学知识为主。进士科相比明经,录取人数少而考试难度大,故当时有"三十老明经,五十少进士"的俗语。白居易登第这一科仅录取17人,他名列第4,而且年龄最小,因此很得意地写下"慈恩塔下题名处,十七人中最少年"的诗句。此后他在长安附近的郊县和中央政府任低级文官,本来仕途还算顺利,但终因批评时政而触犯权贵,屡遭贬谪,辗转于江州、忠州、杭州、苏州等地任地方官,直到55岁以后才回朝任职,最后以刑部尚书的职位(相当于今天的公安部长)退休,度过一个平静的晚年。

作为一位官员,白居易虽然也秉持道义,恪尽职守,做了许多利国利民的事，但他在当时的名声主要是靠文学获得的。其诗作的最大特点，就是具有能被普通读者欣赏的通俗性。传说他每有新诗写成，都会让家里的老年女性读一读，如果她们读不懂，就加以修改，直到她们能读懂为止。由于他的诗作通俗易懂，在社会上流传极广。据他在致友人元稹(779—831)的信中说，"自长安抵江西三四千里，凡乡校、佛寺、逆旅、行舟之中，往往有题仆诗者；士庶、僧徒、孀妇、处女之口，每有咏仆诗者"。有一个军官要纳一妓女为妾，妓夸耀说："我能背诵白学士的《长恨歌》，怎能和其他人一样！"由是身价大增。传说新罗国的商人将白居易诗带回国，卖给首相，一篇能得一百两银子，若有假冒都能被辨认出来。白居易去世后，唐宣宗(810—859)也作诗悼念他，中有"童子解吟《长恨》曲，胡儿能唱《琵琶》篇"两句，足见白居易的作品流传之广和受世人欢迎的程度。

在白居易之前，文人的作品多是由学生或后裔编集的，白居易是现知第一位自己编集作品的诗人。他一生曾三次编集自己的作品，每次都留下一篇编后记，说明作品的写作和保存情况。现在他的诗作留下 2,740 多首，是唐代诗人中存诗最多的一位，当然也是诗作保存得最完整的一位。从他留下的诗歌和文章中，我们可以了解这位诗人的生活、情感和思想观念，看到他的政治立场和行政才能。他丰富的诗文作品可以说是唐代中叶政治生态、社会生活和文人境遇的一面镜子，他毕生的所为成为古代文人处世哲学的典范，而他独特的艺术风格也开辟了以后诗歌中日常生活审美化的道路。

白居易秉持儒家"穷则独善其身，达则兼济天下"的处世原则，在谏官之任敢于言事，勇于批评朝政的缺失。同时又抱着"文章合为时而著，歌诗合为事而作"的信念，用诗歌的形式书写时事，议论当时的社会问题，其鲜明的纪实性甚至具备了新闻传媒的属性，犀利的文辞使被批评的权贵、军阀坐立不安。在遭受打击被贬谪外放后，白居易远离政治漩涡，明哲保身，转而以享受日常生活之闲适，追求诗酒征逐的友朋宴乐为归宿。这种"志在兼济，行在独善，奉而始终之则为道，言而发明之则为诗"，顺应时势调整自己行为模式的人生态度，后来一直为文人们所仿效，白居易也因此成为中国古代文人的精神偶像之一。

元和十年(815)，白居易首次编集自己的作品，将 800 多首诗分为 4 类：讽喻诗、感伤诗、闲适诗、杂律诗。据他自己解释，讽喻诗是议论时事的作品，闲适诗是吟咏闲情逸致的作品，感伤诗是朋友往来、感于人事升沉的作品，其他不易归类的各种体式之作就归入杂律诗。现在看来，闲适和感伤两类之间，时有题材、主题相似之处,很难截然区别。学者推测很可能是这两类诗针对的读者不同,闲适诗是面对一般读者的,而感伤诗是只给自己亲近的朋友看的。事实上,白居易清楚地意识到自己的写作动机与当时阅读趣味的差距。他对诗友元稹说:"我的诗,人们所喜欢的,不过是杂律诗和《长恨歌》之类罢了。他们看重的,恰恰是我自己轻视的。像讽喻诗那样的激烈批评,闲适诗那样的平淡无奇,难免质朴或迂阔,世人不喜欢也是很自然的。"但后人却不这么看,反而对讽喻诗和闲适诗大加推崇:认为《新乐府》一类的讽喻诗描绘了唐王朝后期社会各阶层的生活状况,抨击了社会存在的不公正现象和政治黑暗的现实;而他的闲适诗则将日常生活场景引入诗中,首开诗歌关注日常生活的风气。

从诗歌史的角度看,白居易诗歌被公认的独创性表现在这样几个方面:(一)扩大作品的篇幅,经常以较长的篇幅叙述更丰富的社会内容。尤其是用七言歌行的体式写成的抒情意味浓厚的叙事诗,实开一代风气,其代表作就是脍炙人口的《长恨歌》和《琵琶行》;(二)关注日常生活,善于捕捉日常生活中的诗意化内容;(三)在七言律诗中发展出一种语法自然、意思浅白、韵律流畅而接近口语的风格;(四)将诗歌作为友朋间情感交流的手段,用次韵(重复对方诗作押韵的字和排列次序)的方式赓和对方的作品。这些特征都对后来的诗歌影响深远。

诗歌发展到白居易的时代,语言和意象的陈熟都到了不得不变革的境地,在"惟陈言之务去"(韩愈,768—824)的意识主导下,诗人们纷纷从不同的角度探索创新的途径。经过诗人们的努力探索,最终形成两个明显的潮流,一是追求奇险怪异的韩愈、孟郊(751—814)诗派,一是追求平易流利的元稹、白居易诗派。前者的目标是超越日常生活,颠覆习惯的感觉秩序,以夸张变形的奇峭风格出新;后者则相反,要回到日常生活,以日常生活的审美化为核心,开辟一种平易近人的诗歌风格。两派竞雄于一时,但几十年后韩孟诗派就趋于式微,而元白诗派绵延不绝,到宋代由苏轼发扬光大,成为一种影响深远的风格范型。

不过,历史的有趣在于,白居易虽然在当时赢得了一般读者的喜爱,他的许多作品脍炙人口,但在宋以后的13世纪后期到17世纪中叶,他却很少受到专业的诗歌评论家的好评。他的平易风格经常被视为浅俗,他日常化的题材经常被视为平庸。直到清初,他在王士禛(1634—1711)、叶燮(1627—1703)、沈德潜(1673—1769)等著名批评家眼里,仍算不上是值得学习的杰出诗人。

白居易的经典化要到清高宗亲自审定《御选唐宋诗醇》才初步实现。

《御选唐宋诗醇》是中国历史上第一部声称由君主御选并撰序的诗歌选集，选录了李白、杜甫、白居易、韩愈、苏轼、陆游六家作为唐、宋诗歌的代表，于乾隆十五年(1750)刊行。在当时，将白居易与李白、杜甫相提并称，完全是出于清高宗乾隆帝个人的诗歌趣味，在乾隆本人留下的庞大诗集中，有和白居易诗20题、元稹诗9题，共111首。乾隆帝将白居易选入《御选唐宋诗醇》，立即引起庙堂臣僚和天下士子的注意。沈德潜所编的著名唐诗选本《唐诗别裁集》，初刊本并未收录白居易诗。等到沈氏看到《御选唐宋诗醇》，马上增补白居易诗，出版重订本。从此，白居易就与李白、杜甫并立于唐代最伟大诗人的行列了。

白居易生前，其诗作就传入了朝鲜半岛，11世纪后高丽朝文人出现模仿白居易的时尚，至今韩国还保存有不少白居易诗集的珍贵版本。白居易诗集在9世纪中叶也传入日本，并获得君臣朝野的喜爱。平安时代著名学者大江维时所编的《千载佳句》，收录中日诗人1,110首诗歌，白居易就占了535首。从9世纪到12世纪的400年里，白居易诗歌不只是作为他国文学杰作被吟咏鉴赏，更作为文学创作的典范被模仿。至今日本国民对白居易诗歌的喜爱仍历久不衰，先后出版的相关注释、评论和研究书籍也相当多。

欧美对白居易诗的接受始于法语翻译。1862年汉学家埃尔维·圣·德尼侯爵翻译出版的《唐诗选》，1867年著名诗人戈蒂耶翻译出版的《玉笛》，都收录了白居易的诗作。英国传教士翟理士于1901年出版的世界上第一部《中国文学史》，其中"唐朝文学"一章也介绍了李白、杜甫、白居易等18位诗人的作品。但真正让西方读者认识白居易的翻译家还是英国学者阿瑟·韦利，他非常喜欢白居易诗，在1918年出版的《一百七十首中国古诗选》中翻译了59首白居易诗，后来又陆续翻译，先后将200多首白居易诗译成英文，并于1949年出版《白居易生平及时代》一书，影响广泛。迄今为止，各种语言的白居易诗歌翻译本已多达200余种，白居易诗歌受到了世界各国读者的喜爱。

本书是赵彦春教授长年从事中国古典文学作品英译的成果之一。赵教授曾先后翻译了《诗经》《论语》《道德经》《庄子》《曹操诗集》《曹丕诗集》《曹植诗集》《李白诗歌全集》《王维诗歌全集》等几十部经典作品，向英语世界介绍中国文学。这次他又挑起了第一部英译《白居易诗歌全集》的重担，让我这个研究中国古典诗歌的学者钦佩不已。而他以诗译诗，以经译经，形神兼顾的要求与方法无疑开启了一个新的范式。我相信他的翻译将架起一座桥梁,让英语世界的读者走进唐代诗人白居易的诗美,领略这位伟大诗人为我们构建的古老而又新鲜的艺术境界。我期待着译著的出版,让我们来分享赵教授阅读、翻译白居易诗歌的愉快经验。

蒋 寅

2020 年 9 月 30 日

Introduction

Dear reader, as you probably know, we Chinese have long seen our country as a nation of poetry, which is our favorite art that is most commonly read and recited. The ability to compose poems was even deemed the most important, and had been the most significant criterion for the hottest and highest Imperial Examination in T'ang (618 - 907). The criterion was once abolished after Sung, but brought back in the 22nd year during Emperor Ch'ien Lung's reign in Ch'ing (1757), rendering poetry composition a must for civil-service candidates. The cultural monopoly of ancient feudalism and the popularity of loving poetry endow emperors, ministers, civil and military officials with the ability to compose poems. Over 40,000 poems written in his whole life, Emperor Highsire Hungli of Ch'ing left us the largest number of poems through ancient times, almost equal to all the poems handed down from T'ang. Besides, officials in the past at all levels from Tribune (Three High Lords) and Prime Minister left countless collections of poems, also a wonder worldwide.

This collection of poems you are about to read were written by Chü-e Pai (772 - 846), the most popular and gifted poet during mid-T'ang. Outstanding talent shown at an early age, he began to compose poems at five or six, and was already familiar with rhythm and rhyme of poetry at nine. As he grew up a young man, he went to Long Peace, the capital, to take the Imperial Examination, and took his poems to visit his predecessor, a famous poet called K'uang Ku (cir. 730 - cir. 806). Ku joked about Pai's name (Chü-e means living easily in Chinese) and said, "It is not easy to live in Long Peace due to high prices!", but as soon as he opened his book of poems and finished reading the first poem *Seeing a Friend Off by an Old*

Grassland, he hurriedly shifted, saying: "Anything could be easy for you, who can compose such a good poem, I was just joking!"

With the recognition of the poetic circle, Chü-e Pai was successfully admitted as an enteree (Chin-shih) at the age of 27 in the 16th year of Right One (Chen Yüan) (800). Enteree and classic reader (Ming Ching) were two main testing subjects in the Imperial Examination of T'ang, with the former mainly focused on literature and the latter mainly focused on classics. Compared with classic readers, fewer enterees were enrolled and it was much harder to be, so there was a saying "It is old to be a classic reader in one's 30s, while young to be an enteree in his 50s". Furthermore, he was the fourth and youngest of the only 17 enrolled, so he proudly wrote a line "Behold the inscription roll of names under Grace Tower, of seventeen he's the youngest in flower". Since then, he had worked as a petty civil official at the suburban counties near Long Peace and the central government, well done in the beginning, but eventually offending the dignitaries by criticizing the politics, hence being relegated several times to work as regional officials in prefectures such as Chiangchou, Chiongchou, Hangchou and Suchou. He did not come back to the central government until 55, and retired as Minister of Justice (equivalent to today's Minister of Public Security), spending his twilight years quietly.

As an official, Chü-e Pai adhered to the principles and duties, contributing a lot to the country and people, however, his fame back then was mainly attained through literature, since the greatest feature of his poems is vernacularism, as could be appreciated by common folks. It was said that whenever he wrote a poem, he would invite elder women in the family to read it. If they failed to understand it, he would revise it until they could. The lucidity of his poems leads to wide spreading. According to a letter he wrote to his friend Chen Yüan (779-831), "During the three or four thousand miles from Long Peace to Chianghsi, there were always my inscriptions for township schools, Buddhist temples, inns or boats; there were always chanters of my poems among gentries or civilians, Buddhist monks, widows or virgins." Once an officer took a prostitute as a concubine, and she boasted, "how could I be treated like others since I could recite Chü-e Pai's *Lasting Grief*?"Therefore, her status was raised. It is said that the merchants of Hsinlo brought Pai's poems back home and sold them to the king for a hundred taels of silver per poem, and any fake ones could be identified. After his death, Emperor Deepsire (810 – 859) of T'ang also memorized him with a poem, including these two lines: "Children could manage to chant *Lasting Grief*; Barbarians could e'en sing *A Pipa Player*", which shows how well liked and popular his works were.

Before Chü-e Pai's time, literati's works were collected by their students or descendants. Pai is known as the first poet to compile his own works. He collected his own three times in his life, each time leaving an afterword explaining how they were written and preserved. At present, with over 2,740 poems, he is the T'ang poet with the most poems left and best preserved. His poems and articles show his life, emotion, ideas, political stance and administrative ability, and his rich legacy of works can be said to be a mirror of the political ecology, social life and literati's situation during mid – T'ang. Besides, his life experiences of being an official and reclusion became a model of ancient literati's life philosophy, while his unique artistic style also opened up aestheticization of daily life in poetry.

Pai adhered to the life principle of Confucianism, "Preserve your dignity as nobody; promote social welfare as somebody". He dared to speak out in the position of an imperial censor and criticize the dereliction of the government, meanwhile holding the belief of "Articles and chapters are written for the time, while songs and poems are written for matters". He wrote about current affairs and discussed social problems in the form of poetry, whose distinctive documentary feature even possessed the property of news media today, and his poignancy set the criticized warlords in terrible fidgets. After being banished or exiled, Pai stayed away from the political whirlpool and worldly affairs, turning to the leisure of daily life and pursuing banquets of poetry and wine with friends. This kind of life attitude, as adjusted his life style in accordance with situations, has been followed by literati all the time. Therefore, he has become one of the spiritual idols of ancient Chinese literati.

In the tenth year of Onecord (Yüanho) (815), Chü-e Pai compiled his own works for the first time, and divided over 800 poems into four categories: allegorical, sentimental, leisurely and miscellaneous. According to his own explanation, allegorical poetry discusses current affairs, leisurely poetry chants leisurely feelings, sentimental poetry expresses friends' come and go, ups and downs of life, and other styles that are not easy to be classified are miscellaneous poetry. Now it seems that there are similarities of theme and content between leisurely and sentimental poems, and difficult to distinguish them. Scholars inferred that it is likely that the two kinds of poems aimed at different readers, with leisurely poems for ordinary readers, sentimental poems for close friends. Actually, Pai was clearly aware of the gap between his writing motivation and reading interests at that time. He said to his friend Chen Yüan: "What people like about my poetry is only the miscellaneous poems, such as *Lasting Grief* and so on. What they value is exactly what I neglect, but it is natural that they do not like the intense criticism of allegorical poetry or the plainness of leisurely poetry since they are inevitably simple and pedantic." However, later generations actually praised his allegorical and leisurely poetry, for that the allegorical poetry like *New Conservatoire* depicted the living conditions of all social classes in late T'ang and attacked the social injustice and the reality of political darkness, and his leisurely poetry introduces scenes of daily life into his poems, and is the first to focus on the atmosphere of daily life.

From the view of poetic history, the acknowledged originality of Pai's poems is shown in the following aspects: (1) Expending the length of the works, he often narrates richer social matter in a larger length, especially very lyric poems written in the style of seven-word song which indeed blazed a trail, representatives being *Lasting Grief* and *A Pipa Player*.

(2) Focusing on daily life and accomplished in capturing the poetics of daily life; (3) Developing a style with natural grammar, simple meaning, smooth rhythm and vernacularism in the poems of seven - word rhythm; (4) Making poetry a means of emotional communication between friends by replying to the rhyming of their works (which means repeating the rhyming words and sequence of a rival or pal's poem). All of these characteristics exert a profound influence on later poetry.

By the time of Pai, the triteness of language and imagery had to be changed. Under the guidance of the consciousness of "to remove the trite language" (Yü Han, 768 - 824), poets were exploring innovative approaches from different perspectives. Through their efforts, two obvious trends were finally formed, one was the pursuit of the bizarre and strange genre represented by Yü Han and Chiao Meng (751 - 814), and the other was the pursuit of the plain and smooth genre represented by Chen Yüan and Chü-e Pai. The former's goal was to transcend daily life, to subvert the habitual sense of order, and to bring out new ideas with exaggerated and distorted style. The latter, on the other hand, returned to daily life and developed an approachable poetic style with the aesthetics of daily life at its core. The two schools competed for influence for a while, but after a few decades, Han and Meng's tended to decline, while Yüan and Pai's prospered, to be carried forward by Shih Su in Sung, becoming a far-reaching model.

However, what is interesting about history is that though Pai won the favor and popularity of common readers, he was rarely praised by professional poetic critics from the late 13th century to the mid-17th century after Sung. His plain style was often dismissed as vulgar, and his daily-life themes as banal. Until the early Ch'ing, Shihchen Wang (1634 - 1711), Hsieh Yeh (1627 - 1703), Tech'ien Shen (1673 - 1769) and other famous critics still did not consider him as an outstanding poet worth learning from. The canonization of Chü-e Pai was not realized until the imperial selection of *T'ang and Sung Mellow Poems* approved by Emperor Highsire of Ch'ing.

The first collection of poems purportedly selected and prefaced by the emperor in Chinese history included Pai Li, Fu Tu, Chü-e Pai, Yü Han, Shih Su and Yu Lu as representatives of T'ang and Sung poems, and was published in 1750 during the reign of Emperor Ch'ienlung. At that time, mentioning Chü-e Pai together with Pai Li and Fu Tu was totally out of Emperor Highsire's personal taste. In his immense collections of poems, there are 111 poems in response to previous poets, 20 subjects to Chü-e Pai and 9 subjects to Chen Yüan, and his selecting Chü-e Pai's poems into the *T'ang and Sung Mellow Poems* immediately attracted the attention of officials and scholars. Pai's poems were not included in the first edition of *Anthology of T'ang Poems* compiled by Tech'ien Shen, and as soon as Shen saw the imperial selection of *T'ang and Sung Mellow Poems*, he supplemented Pai's poems instantly and published a revised edition. From then on, Chü-e Pai, Pai Li and Fu Tu were among the greatest poets of T'ang.

Pai's poems were introduced to Korean Peninsula before his death. After 11th century, there was a fashion among Korean literati to imitate Chü-e Pai, and many precious versions of his works are still preserved in South Korea now. Pai's poetry was also introduced to Japan in the middle of the 9th century and favored by emperors and officials. *Best Verse in a Thousand Years*, compiled by the famous scholar Kolo Toki in Heian Era, contains 1,110 poems by Chinese and Japanese poets, among which Pai's account for 535. During the 400 years from 9th century to 12th century, Chü-e Pai's poems were not only recited and appreciated as masterpieces of foreign literature in Japan, but also imitated as models of literary creation. Till now, Japanese are still fond of Pai's poems and have published quite a number of annotated and research books on his poems.

The acceptance of Chü-e Pai's poems in Europe and America began with French translation. *The Selected T'ang Poetry*, translated and published by the Sinologist Le Marquis de Saint-Denis in 1862, and *Jade Flute*, translated and published by the famous poet Gautier in 1867, both including Chü-e Pai's poems. The first *Literary History of China* in the world, published in 1901 by the British missionary Lishih Chai, in which the Chapter T'ang Literature also introduces the works of 18 poets including Pai Li, Fu Tu and Chü-e Pai. But the translator that really enabled western readers to know Chü-e Pai is the British scholar Arthur Waley, who was very fond of Chü-e Pai's poetry, and translated 59 of Pai's poems in *One Hundred and Seventy Selected Ancient Chinese Poems* published in 1918, then, he translated more than two hundred Chü-e Pai's poems into English successively, and published *Chü-e Pai's Life and Era*, with a profound effect in 1949. Up to now, there have been more than 200 translated versions of Chü-e Pai's poems in various languages, and his poems are favored by readers worldwide.

This book is one of the fruitful achievements of Professor Yanchun Chao who has been engaged in the English translation of Chinese classics for many years. Professor Chao has translated dozens of classics, including *The Book of Songs*, *Analects*, *The Word and the World*, *Sir Lush*, *Ts'ao Ts'ao's Poems*, *Ts'ao P'i's Poems*, *Ts'ao Chih's Poems*, *A Complete Edition of Pai Li's Poems in Chinese and English*, and *A Complete Edition of Wei Wang's Poems* in Chinese and English and so on, introducing Chinese literature and leading them to go global. This time he takes on the arduous task of *A Complete Edition of Chü-e Pai's Poems* in Chinese and English, which surprises me, a scholar of classics Chinese poetry, so much so that I cannot but truly admire him. His requirement and method of translating Poesie into Poesie and Classic into Classic with an emphasis on form and meaning tension will undoubtedly open up a new paradigm. I believe that his translation will be a bridge for global readers to access the poetic charm of a T'ang poet, Chü-e Pai, and to appreciate the ancient and fresh artistic realm that this great poet constructed for us. I'm looking forward to its publication so that you could share the pleasure with me of reading Professor Chao's translation of Chü-e Pai's poems.

Yin Chiang

2020.9.30

译者自序

问你：哪个朝代的诗歌最伟大？你可能毫不犹豫：唐朝。要问你谁是唐朝最伟大的诗人，你可能不好回答，因为有好几位难以取舍。如果不选冠亚军而推举几位出类拔萃者便容易得多。王维、李白、杜甫、白居易无疑是最优秀的，他们造就了唐诗的高峰。

这一高峰地球人应该有足够的认识，然而翻译绝非易事，而且误区颇多。最核心的是"道"的缺失。

"形而上者谓之道，形而下者谓之器。"这是《易经》对人类一切知识体系的高度而精准的概括，是人类知识的坐标系，是人类智慧的坐标系。然而，西方启蒙时代打开了思想的"潘多拉的盒子"，将"道"瓦解于无形——诚如《论语》所言："天下之无道也久矣。"在西方学术出现了多次转向之后，中华传统文化的复兴已然发生——集结号已经吹响，"道"的光辉已出现于东方的地平线上。

人类思想的大变革、大繁荣大多肇始于翻译——比如东方的佛经翻译、西方的《圣经》翻译，以及近代以来的西学东渐所带动的种种翻译。中华经典外译始于明朝末年，译者多是西方汉学家、外交家和教会人士。清朝末年以后出现了一些华人译者。

但我们遗憾地发现，诗性的中国经典和诗本身的神采在很大程度上被遮蔽了，正应了罗伯特·弗罗斯特那句话：诗就是翻译中丢掉的东西。

在诸多类别的翻译实践中，文学翻译是最复杂、最难以应对的一种类型，而诗歌翻译又是文学翻译中最值得关注的对象。

人是诗性的存在；诗是人类的家园；诗是人类的表征。作诗与译诗都是以诗来表征我们自身，来表征我们的世界。诗的文学特性在于以有形的文字铺排映现无形的灵魂的跃动。"有形"表现为诗的文字载体或织体特征以及押韵、节奏构成的格律，"无形"即意外之意。诗应和着宇宙的递归性，可表现为符号之符号，它表达意义，又表达意义之意义，言有尽而意无穷。

中国是诗的国度。历史的遗存可以追溯到黄帝时代的《弹歌》。《弹歌》是二字格，是四言体的先驱。四言体古诗在公元前六世纪盛行，随之骚体诗、五言体古诗、七言体古诗和杂言古诗相继成型；进入唐朝，中华民族迎来了诗歌大繁荣，出现五言律体诗、七言律体诗和六言律体诗。

唐朝（公元618—907年）是盛世中的盛世，文学艺术在唐朝达到鼎盛，尤其是在诗歌方面达到了中国文学的巅峰。关于唐朝有多少诗人以及他们写了多少首诗，今人已无法统计，清朝编纂的《全唐诗》共收录四万九千四百零三首，所涉作者共有二千八百七十三人。仅从这些遗存，我们也可以看到唐代文人以体量巨大的诗歌记录了文人风骨和浩荡的盛唐气象。王维、李白、杜甫、白居易无疑是唐朝灿如明珠的诗人中最为耀眼的四人。闲逸如"诗佛"王维，寄情山水，禅意尽见于遣词造句中。浪漫如"诗仙"李白，才情恣意挥洒于诗行间；深刻、沉郁如现实主义诗人杜甫，忧国忧民之思倾注在一字一句中；真诚、清醒如白居易，所思所感皆可见于诗行。四人所作唐诗传世甚多，各领风骚，向后人展示了大唐气象和时代特征。这四位诗人能够代表中国诗歌的高度，在世界文学中也享有崇高的地位。为此，我觉得很有必要把他们留下的六千首诗完整地译成英诗。

西方最早大力进行唐诗英译的是18世纪英国汉学家、诗人詹尼斯（S. Jenyns），译作有《唐诗三百首选读》（*Selections from the 300 Poems of the Tang Dynasty*）和《唐诗三百首选读续集》（*A Further Selections from the 300 Poems of the Tang Dynasty*）。小畑薰良（S. Obata）最早英译了唐代诗人专集，比如1922年在纽约出版的《李白诗集》（*The Works of Li Po, the Chinese Poet*）。其他为唐诗英译做出贡献的英译家还有戴维斯爵士、翟理斯、理雅各、韦利、柳无忌、欧文等等。反观国内，自二十世纪八十年代以来，我国学者、翻译家翻译的唐诗译本有杨宪益与戴乃迭（Gladys）合译的《唐宋诗文选译》（*Poetry and Prose of the Tang and Song*）、徐忠杰翻译的《唐诗二百首新译》（*200 Chinese Tang Poems in English Verse*）、王守义与诺弗尔（J. Neville）合译的《唐宋诗词英译》（*Poems from Tang and Song Dynasties*）、吴钧陶翻译的《杜甫诗英译（一百五十首）》（*Tu Fu One Hundred and Fifty Poems*）、许渊冲翻译的《唐诗三百首新译》（*English-Chinese 300 Tang Poems A New Translation*）、《李白诗选译》（*Selected Poems of Li Bai*）、《唐诗一百五十首英译》（*150 Tang Poems*）等。可见，唐诗的英译版本虽然相对较多，然文言文的晦涩和唐诗独有的文学性为唐诗英译设置了重重障碍，回顾现有的翻译作品，唐诗英译成果并不成系统，译本多零散且译文质量参差不齐，偏离原文甚远，自然传播效果也不甚理想。本该灿如明星的唐诗反而由于翻译的精准程度不匹配而被拉下神坛，中华文化的神采在译文中被遮蔽、被消解。远游的诗神是一个蒙灰的形象，哲学内涵也被误解、被埋没。在当代文明大潮交汇的新形势下，唐诗英译亟待寻求新的翻译方法论作为指导，亟须开辟新思路以走出困局。

翻译虽然基本上表现于文字转换，实质上却蕴含着大学之道。翻译始终以言语系统之间的"易"即言语单位的切换与调变来传情达意，同时也以其与宇宙之间的全息律（holographics）表征着"davar""Brahma""道"。翻译是不乏理论的，但纵观形形色色的西方翻译理论，由于没有形而上的统领和关照，其认识是庞杂的、肤浅的、碎片化的，甚至有的理论竟是颠覆本原、本质以借翻译理论之名行解构翻译理论之实，而传统的准则，比如忠实、对等，乃至文本本身都成了负面的模因而被解构了，翻译成了是其所非的荒谬和无所不是的弥散。

笔者 2005 年著《翻译学归结论》一书，逆西方潮流而动，以《周易》为指向，从众说纷纭的混沌中祭出一个明确的范式，这是摆脱混乱和无定的一个企图。它说：翻译是一个由原则统领的、译者借此进行参数调变与否决的动态系统。由此，译/易的本质是类比的、可拓逻辑的，即化矛盾为不矛盾，变不可译为可译。正如唐朝的贾公彦云："译即易。谓换易言语使相解也。"语言符号是对抽象语义的表征，无论采取何种表征方式，只要能达到对等的目的即可。翻译的最根本的目的是要传递原汁原味的原文精髓，这绝不是改写，不是操控，更不是通过直译、意译或零翻译就能解决的。它需要译者设身处地，体会原作者的审美情调和意图，通过合理有效的调控，使译文最大限度地贴近原文，最大限度地实现形美、音美和意美的有机统一，即实现译文中各个变量间的平衡与相互制约，使译文自给自足，达致善译。译文虽然在语形和语义上与原文有所差别，但在意旨上又和原文保持高度一致。

自提出翻译学归结论后，笔者在典籍外译实践中就始终以翻译学归结论为理论指导，坚守悬置法则（ceteris paribus rule）即其他条件等同（other things being equal）下的语码转换。大道至简，这是最高效的方法论的起点。在其外围便是翻译生态——翻译伴随翻译生态环境而生。翻译与生态环境，犹如阴阳两种力量，相摩相荡，相生相克，交感成和，生生不息。

具体到诗歌翻译而言，诗的"有形"与"无形"为诗歌翻译带来了避无可避的翻译困境。在中西方诗歌体裁中，诗可以分为散体诗和格律诗两大类：散体诗强调自然、不拘束；格律诗是一种编排，照应生命的律动，在严谨中书写诗意，天各一方的民族还不约而同地造就了格律。世界范围内，英汉诗歌又占据世界诗歌的大半。英诗的格律由四种基调格（抑扬格、扬抑格、抑抑扬格和扬抑抑格）、两种变格（抑抑格和扬扬格）和不同音步数组合而成，再辅以交替韵、搂抱韵和重叠韵构成多种经典诗体。汉语古诗则以极富乐感的方块字写成，它的格律主要涉及四个方面，即押韵、节奏、平仄和歌唱或吟诵行为，通过押韵和平仄实现古诗的表情达意，或热烈欢快，或文静雅致。格律诗的诗体特征之鲜明，直接造成格律诗翻译的壁障。即使诗歌翻译艰难如此，就格律诗的翻译而言，我也是绝不含糊的——这样的诗不允许含糊，此乃格律之谓也。

虽说诗无达诂、译无定法，译者在翻译诗歌时也不可过度夸大主观能动性，更不可任意妄为、随意解构，诗人的思想性和诗的文学性需得到足够的重视，译诗必须为诗。诗歌翻译首先要受到押韵、节奏这一形式因素的制约，甚至说还要满足演唱并可以适当发挥的需要。当然，这只是一个显性的要求。为保证作品的品位，语言、美学、哲学等层面的隐性因素都需要全盘考虑。笔者近年来着力进行典籍英译，其中一大类别就是中国古代诗歌英译。在翻译时，我始终践行的翻译原则就是"以诗译诗，译经如经，是其所是"。

译诗是高度辩证的制衡机制与审美行为。关于翻译标准，我认为：所谓辩证，它是不忠而忠、不等而等的调配；所谓制衡，它是依权重而逐层否决的仲裁；所谓审美，它是以可视、可感、可唱、可听的意象营造而直入心境。翻译必须被赋予一定的自由度。译者可以根据目的或意图的需要，在不影响大体的前提下增加译文的可读性或可唱性，甚至必要时可以做些许改动或牺牲，这样反而能使译文符合原文的初衷。翻译虽然多变，但绝不是没有标准，只是它的标准不是机械的、僵死的、一成不变的，它的最高标准其实就一个字：美。

译好一首诗或一部作品首先要统摄原文要旨和神采，然后用另一种文字恰如其分地再现。何谓再现？再现不是字词的简单对应而是语篇的功能对等——译文与原文在逻辑关系、审美构成和语用意图等各个层面的对应。可见，在诗歌翻译中，逼近原则是首要的——这是翻译及评判的起点和根据；逼近的同时也为达到最佳效果进行灵活调变，以直译尽其可能，意译按其所需的辩证性为旨归。

翻译中国古代诗歌尤其是格律诗时，秉承着"以诗译诗"的翻译原则，笔者首先就要"保留"格律，绝不能以"自由"为托词对其格律任意阉割而损伤诗美。当然，我也不提倡因声损义的凑韵，或为了押韵而把句子搞得怪里怪气，这比平庸还低廉。韵律来自语义或语境，它是构成织综的重要成分，与之不可分割——分割了就不是这首诗了。它服务于整体效果，牵一发而动全身。具体来说，"译诗如诗"即译者在认识到诗的形式是诗的格式或模板的基础上，首先有必要对译文在形式上进行限定。译为无韵的散文体或有韵的参差不一的诗行不符合我的审美取向。译诗虽然无强制性的要求，但在实践中也能提取出便于操作和评估的一般准则。比如英语的一个音步一般为两个音节，而五个音步一般为十个音节，与汉语的七言在形式和内容上可以达到最佳匹配。所以为了便于操作我做了类比性的设定：将汉语三言类比为五音节；将汉语四言类比为六音节；将汉语五言类比为八音节；将汉语六言类比为九音节；将汉语七言类比为十音节；将汉语八言类比为十二音节；将汉语九言类比为十四音节。

其次，由于英汉诗歌中韵诗又占绝大比例，在译汉语韵诗时，译诗也必须押韵且有节奏，"以诗译诗，是其所是"在翻译韵诗时就包括"以韵译韵"，这一点不能妥协，但如何押韵以及采用何种韵式则可以由译者自己调整。由于韵或韵式都是类比的，除了特殊的诗体，译诗中的韵式可以相对灵活。我多用偶韵和交叉韵或隔行韵；英诗绝大部分都是抑扬格，也会根据表意的需要夹杂扬抑格、抑抑扬格、扬抑抑格等，译诗也会求诸此类格律。在英译过程中，始终注重翻译的形意张力，避免因韵害义，同时又保证原诗风格的完整再现及诗歌情感、意境、意象等内涵的高度传达，最大化地实现翻译的效度与信度。英诗的格律不像中国的格律诗那样严格，总的原则是音韵和谐。好的译诗必须是不蔓不枝，自然天成的。

再者，除了对诗体、诗韵的保留与再现手段，中国古代诗歌翻译的另一重难点在于对文化名词的翻译处理。中华文化是一个复杂的大系统，内涵深厚，博大精深，可分为形形色色的模块，比如梅兰竹菊、琴棋书画、三皇五帝、三纲五常都是特定文化的产物。并且同一名词在不同文化语境中能够呈现不一样的内涵，中华风物可被赋予不同的内容。在中国古代诗歌英译实践中，一个负责任的译者不可忽视对这类名词的内涵和意义的解释和传达，因为翻译的目的就是不同文明之间的理解互通。对文化名词的妙用往往能体现并塑造文人的个人风格，李白的浪漫主义诗风瑰丽绚烂，白居易、杜甫等诗人的现实主义诗风发人深省，王维的田园山水诗风清新脱俗。译诗也重在译味(translating the taste)。如果仅是简单地释义，这便不是文学翻译而是文字翻译。因此，好的译诗也当一如原诗，文本自足，同时与原文的文学风格最大限度地映现。

  对于在英语中无法完全找到对等表达的汉语文化名词时，笔者选择了以注释的形式扩展相关知识。不过，对于译文而言，注释属于副文本(paratext)即独立于译文的另一个文本，背景知识就语篇而言是缺省值(default value)，尽管在一定程度上也会影响读者对文本的认知，但对于正文而言不是文本的必要成分，它只是揭示本族语者可能具有的默认知识。而对于英语读者而言，注释却可以在不影响译诗结构和表达的条件下，成为可辅助英语读者理解译文的、有效且必要的文本。作注和译诗是不同的路径，译者不需要想象，不需要发挥，不需要浪漫，但需要查阅、考证、取舍和提炼；同时译者还要借鉴最近的考古发现，如此才能做到用最简练的语言来概括某一注释所需的完整的历史文化要素。对译者而言，作注还能再次验证译文的准确程度，起到查漏、勘误作用，反过来提高翻译质量。

  在翻译和作注的过程中，译者对于专有名词必然有很多纠结，担心信息会有所遗漏、扭曲或冗余。笔者认为：为了保全原文信息和可读性，译者在翻译中应尽量避免音译；即便音译，也要照顾西方的阅读习惯，可采用西方读者和海外华人熟悉的威氏拼音；更重要的是翻译要避免编码的夹生，比如中国文化的层级体系的编码是从大至小，而英语则是从小至大，比如"蓝田山石门精舍"译成英语则应该把"蓝天山"的译文置后，如 Stonegate Vihara at Mt. Blue Field，而译作 at Mt. Blue Field Stonegate Vihara 则怪异。同理，"李白"姓李名白，译作"Li Pai"就违反了英语的编码规律，正如把"卡尔·马克思"译作"马克思·卡尔"那样悖谬，而译作"Pai Li"才符合英语的规范。

  对于有些特有的中华文化概念如精卫、后羿、颛顼、秀才等，如果音译过滤掉了中国文化的特有意义。译者还需要基于汉语词源和英语构词法在译文中进行合理创译，仿拟汉语的构词法，尽力把词素所表达的意义译出来，这等于向英语输入词汇，利用词汇在文化系统中的互文性，从而帮助英语读者通过上下文推断该词的意义所指。比如"秀才"译作"xiu cai"或"hsiu ts'ai"对于英文读者而言是毫无意义的，而重新编码为"showcharm"，读者则可以产生相应的联想，而随着认知语境的增强，则可以达到等同于原文的认知效果。通过以上翻译策略，译诗可以尽可能保留原诗用典情况，并用脚注形式注释其中出现的历史典故、神话传说、文化习俗等，使读者能够迅速了解诗歌中的典故及文化内涵。可见，注释文本为达成文化互通这一翻译的最终目的也起到了积极的推手作用，一定程度上弥补了语言系统客观差异所带来的文化缺省的难解现象。

言而总之，译者如若在中国古代诗歌英译实践中，贯彻"以诗译诗，是其所是"和逼近原则，尽可能在诗体、诗韵上做到还原和再现，且以注释辅助文化名词的翻译，译诗才能一如原文，做到浅而不白、质而不俗，达成形美、意美、音美的辩证统一，这便逼近等值、等效了。如此说来，在诗歌翻译实践中，译文比肩乃至超越原文是可能的——这取决于如何操控"言尽意"与"言不尽意"的悖论和如何破解翻译的斯芬克斯之谜。

目前放眼译界，译者由于欠缺形而上的元理论意识，对翻译本体论以及语言本体论认识不足，同时欠缺语言各分相学科的系统知识，大多还拘泥于话语层次的静态的语码转换，其译文难免失真、异化。纵观典籍外译，翻译之敝不仅遮蔽了中华文化的神采而且还割裂了中西文化一体性，不仅没能促进文明互通，反而还弄巧成拙，造成更大的"隔阂"。

笔者基于对翻译本体论和语言本体论的深刻认识，以扎实的中华文化经典英译实践为佐证，提出：典籍外译新局面的突破口在于方法论的革新。译者须从翻译本体论出发，将词源学、句法学、语义学乃至哲学、神学等领域融会贯通，突破机械的二元论，以整全的、全息的眼光审察翻译这一悖论性的辩证系统，系统调和可译/不可译等矛盾，在形意张力逼近与趋同当中追求文化、文本的自恰，以期翻译理论的涅槃，使经典外译焕发勃勃生机。

受惠于中华文化复兴这个伟大时代所提供的机遇，我们拥有了便于利用的知识宝库，而国学双语研究也进入了新境界，促进了经典文化翻译的创新。在此背景下，笔者多年来一直思考翻译理论的创新并付诸翻译实践。笔者希望王维、李白、杜甫、白居易的英译可以展示唐诗的面貌，也希望与笔者已出版的其他中华文化典籍和诗歌的英译作品形成呼应，继续提供经得起海内外读者检验、品读的系列译作，为中华文化"走出去"尽一份绵薄之力。

赵彦春

2020 年 9 月 1 日

于上海大学

Introduction by the Translator

If asked which dynasty is the greatest in poetry, you may reply without hesitation: the T'ang dynasty; if further asked who is the greatest poet in the T'ang dynasty, you may feel it uneasy to answer, because there are several too hard to rank. If not required to list the first or second but the best ones, it is much easier. Wei Wang, Pai Li, Fu Tu and Chü-e Pai, no doubt, are among the best. It is they who made the pinnacle of T'ang poetry.

This pinnacle should be well known to all earthlings. But translation is never an easy task and not without traps and fallacies. The most crucial of all is the loss of the Word.

"What is high above is the Word; what is down below is the vessel." This is a detached and exact recapitulation by *The Book of Changes* of the whole system of human knowledge, a coordinate of human knowledge and a coordinate of human wisdom. However, the Enlightenment in the West opened the Pandora's Box of thought and disintegrated the Word into dirt, as is said in *Analects*, "The world has gone astray from the Word for long." While after many turns in the West's academics, the renaissance of traditional Chinese culture has started off. The call to action has been tooted and the dawning of the Word has touched the horizon with a streak of red.

In a large sense, the great revolution or great prosperity of human thought began with translation, for example, the translation of Buddhist scriptures in the East, the translation of the Bible in the West and other kinds of translation brought about by the Eastward Spread of Western Culture in the modern era. The translation of Chinese classics started in the late Ming dynasty and translators at that time were mainly sinologists, diplomats and missionaries, and in the late Ching dynasty, some Chinese translators joined in this undertaking.

Unfortunately, we have come to find that the charm of poetic Chinese classics and poetry itself have been eclipsed to a very large extent, which happens to correspond to Robert Frost's dictum, "Poetry is what gets lost in translation."

Of all kinds of translation practice, literary translation is the trickiest and most complicated, and poetry translation is the most noteworthy kind of translation of all literary genres.

Humans are poetic beings, and poetry is the homeland of humans as well as a representation of humans. Poetry creation and poetry translation are both means of representing ourselves and representing our world. The literariness of poetry is a matter of mapping between the arrangement of visible words and the movement of invisible human souls: its visibility is manifested in what we can see, like words, texture and prosody formed by rhythm and rhyme; its invisibility refers to the meaning out of meaning. Poetry is in correspondence with the recursion of the universe and is embodied as a chain of signs or a sign of signs; it expresses meaning, and even expresses the meaning of meaning. As an old saying goes, words are finite but the meaning beyond words is infinite.

China is a nation of poetry. Its history of poetry can date back to *Song of the Catapult* in the age of Lord Yellow. *Song of the Catapult*, two characters or two syllables a line, is a forerunner of the four-character verse, i.e., verse of four characters or four syllables a line. The four-character verse flourished in the sixth century B.C., and then more types of verse came into being, such as the Woebegone form, the five-character old verse, the seven-character old verse and the varying-character old verse. The T'ang dynasty ushered in a golden age of poetry, when there appeared metrical poems with five characters a line, six characters a line and seven characters a line.

The T'ang dynasty (A.D. 618 – A.D. 907) is the most golden period among all golden times, the pinnacle of achievements in Chinese literature and arts, especially in poetry. In regard of the quantity of poets and poems in T'ang, there is no exact number yet. While it can be seen from *A Complete Collections of T'ang Poems*, a book compiled in the Ching dynasty, there are 49,403 poems produced by 2,873 poets in the T'ang dynasty. From these remains, we can also see that litterateurs then showed their charm and recorded the magnificence of that great age in a great multitude of poems. Wei Wang, Pai Li, Fu Tu and Chü-e Pai are, no doubt, the brightest representative figures of all pearl-like poets in the T'ang dynasty. Detached and delighted in nature, Wei Wang pursued the great Word through wording line by line; romantic and unrestrained, Pai Li implanted his sentiments and talents into poetic lines; incisive and realistic, Fu Tu showed his worries over the nation and people in his poems; sober and percipient, Chü-e Pai expressed his great concerns over his kin, friends and homeland. Their abounding poems, though distinctive in style, altogether mirror the history in different stages of that age. These four poets can represent the pinnacle of Chinese poetry and should have been given a stature in world literature. For this reason, I think it necessary to render their poems, 6,000 in total, into English.

The first sinologist who took pains to translate T'ang poetry is S. Jenyns, a British poet in the eighteenth century, with the fruition of *Selections from the 300 Poems of the Tang Dynasty* and *A Further Selections from the 300 Poems of the Tang Dynasty*. The first one to translate the collected works of a T'ang poet is S. Obata, renowned for *The Works of Li Po, the Chinese Poet* published in New York in 1922. Other pioneers are Sir Davis, H. Giles, J. Legge, A. Waley, Wu-chi Liu, Owen and so on. Chinese translators began to translate T'ang poetry in the 1980s, and representative translated works include *Poetry and Prose of the Tang and Song* by Hsien-e Yang and Gladys Yang, *200 Chinese Tang Poems in English Verse* by Chungchieh Hsu, *Poems from Tang and Song Dynasties* by Shou-e

Wang and J. Neville, *Tu Fu One Hundred and Fifty Poems* by Chunt'ao Wu, *English-Chinese 300 Tang Poems: A New Translation* by Yüanch'ung Hsu, *Selected Poems of Li Bai* by Yüanch'ung Hsu, and *150 Tang Poems* by Yüanch'ung Hsu. As it can be seen, the obscurity of classical Chinese writings and the unique literariness of T'ang poems set many obstacles for the translation of T'ang poetry, existing translated works, though in a relatively large quantity, are far from ideal in quality and are fragmented rather than systematic in scale. So, these translations, too far away from their originals in form and meaning, have resulted in an obviously poor communication effect worldwide by now. T'ang poetry that should have been as luminous as bright stars is now being pulled down from its summit by bad translations, and the glory of Chinese civilization gets dimmed and diminished by bad translations. It also means that the images of Chinese Muses travelling afar are covered with a veil of dust, and that Chinese philosophy has been misunderstood and undermined. Against the background of cultural exchanges, a new methodology is in dire need to guide the rendering of T'ang poetry into English, so that translators can find a way out of the current plight.

Translation, a process of text transformation by and large, has an implication in the Word of the universe. It always includes the transformation between two linguistic systems to convey meanings and express emotions, and also mirrors the universal holographics to represent "davar", "Brahma" or the Word. Though there is no lack of translation theories, we can find no directions from metaphysics for translation studies in Western translation theories. The viewpoints expressed in the so-called theories can be judged as sprawling, shallow and fragmented. Some of them have even overthrown the thing-in-itself of translation and have actually deconstructed the basics of translation. Classic norms such as fidelity, equivalence and the text itself are regarded as negative memes and are deconstructed. Translation has run into a state of what it is not, with the dispersion of its essence into being anything but itself.

In 2005, I published a book *A Reductionist Approach to Translatology*, a book that goes in the opposite direction of Western translation theories. With the guidance of *The Book of Changes*, the book aims to set a clear paradigm out of all current chaos and melee, trying to lead translation studies out of disorder. As it proposes, translation is a dynamical system guided by principles, and translators can take advantage of the mechanism of checks and balances to modulate and veto parameters in the process. Hence, the essence of "trans" conforms to analogy and extenic logic, which means converting contradictoriness into compatibility and untranslatability into translatability. Just as the T'ang Confucian Scholar Kungyen Chia put it, "'yi' (falling tone, meaning trans) is equal to 'yi' (falling tone, meaning changing), namely changing from one parole into another to ensure mutual understanding". Linguistic symbols are just representations of abstract semantic meanings, and all representations can reach the same goal, different they may be. The fundamental purpose of translation is to convey the quintessence of the source text in an original way; and definitely, it is not merely what rewriting or manipulation can achieve, and even far beyond the scope of what is called literal translation, free translation or zero translation. According to *A Reductionist Approach to Translatology*, translators are required to be empathetic enough to comprehend the original's aesthetic perception and intention, and then to reasonably modulate parameters to make the translations approximate to the original as much as possible, so that the beauty in form, sound and meaning can be achieved to the largest extent, that is to say, checks and balances among all variables can be realized, and self-consistent as well as high-quality translations can be produced. Translations, though still different from the original in linguistic symbols, are very likely to be highly consistent with it in semantic meaning and motif.

Since the establishment of the reductionist approach to translatology, it has been the theoretical guide throughout my translation practice, especially that of Chinese classics, abiding by the ceteris paribus rule, namely, transcoding in the condition of other things being equal, and insisting that the great Word is the simplest and is the starting point of a methodology of the highest efficiency. Besides, translation also concerns outer communicative environment, in other words, translation exists, concurrent with it. Translation and the communicative environment, just like the two forces Shine and Shade, which endlessly collide with each other, reinforce each other and counteract each other, two in one and united in one.

In terms of poetry, its visible and invisible poetic features bring inevitable obstacles to translation. Chinese poetry and Western poetry can be generally classified into free verse and rhythmic verse. The former highlights naturalness and freedom in verse, while the latter is a fruit of many nations though far apart, featuring rhythmic rules to represent the rhythm of life itself and the poetic atmosphere behind this restriction of rhythmic rules. Chinese poetry and Western poetry can boast of more than half of all poems ever produced. In respect of Western poetry, there are basic meter patterns including four basic meter patterns (Iambus, Trochee, Anapaest and Dactyl) and two variant meter patterns (Pyrrhic and Spondee), metrical foot patterns and three common rhyming schemes (alternate rhyme as abab, enclosing rhyme as abba and distich as aa), which are the most adopted classical patterns. As for Chinese poetry, it is written in Chinese characters characterized by musicality, and the rhythmic verse features in four aspects, that is, rhyming, rhythm, tone pattern (piânn-tseh) and its chanting style for poets to convey meanings and express emotions, ardent or refined. These clear-cut poetic features of metrical verses directly challenge translators. Despite the difficulty and complexity, I show no perfunctoriness, and perfunctoriness is not allowed in metrical verses.

Admitting that "no final interpretation for literary texts, no definite translation of them either", while translating poetry, translators should not over-exaggerate their initiative, let alone wantonly interpreting and deconstructing original texts. An author's ideology and the literariness of a poem should be given enough emphasis, and its translation should still be a poem in itself. Poetry translation is firstly subject to the need of representing the original's poetic forms like rhyming and rhythm, and then to the needs of chanting or other purposes. Certainly, the requirements above are just overt ones, and to ensure the literariness of the original in the translation, invisible connotations of language, philosophy and aesthetics should all be considered. For years I have been devoted to English translation of Chinese classics, ancient poetry in particular. The ultimate translation principle I have long implemented is "translating poesie into poesie and classic into classic, translating it as it is".

Poetry translation is a highly dialectical system of checks and balances and an aesthetic activity. Speaking of translation criteria, as I see it, being dialectical lies in the modulation of parameters for dynamic fidelity and equivalence through seeming infidelity and in equivalence; checks and balances requires translators to decide whether an element should be preferred or sacrificed layer by layer based on its right weight; in aesthetic terms, poetry translation is expected to create visual and acoustical poetic imagery to impress readers. Translators should be given some independence, hence enabled to enhance the readability of a translated text according to pragmatic purposes without affecting the overall arrangements, and even to change or sacrifice some elements, if necessary, to better represent the original's intention. Translation, though ever-changing in the process, can never do without criteria, and criteria should not be mechanical, rigid or immutable. Its highest standard actually is just one word: beauty.

To produce a quality translation of poetry or literature in general, translators firstly need to fully comprehend the original's motif and style, and then appropriately represent it in another language. What is representation? It is not simple word-to-word equivalence but functional or dynamic equivalence in terms of discourse, namely, the equivalence of the original and the translated text in layers such as logical relationship, aesthetic component and pragmatic intention. This shows that in poetry translation, the principle of proximity is primary, which is the starting point and the basis for translation practice and translation criticism. Translators can flexibly modulate elements to achieve the best possible effect, aiming at the maxim "as literal as is possible, as free as necessary".

When translating ancient Chinese poetry, especially Chinese metrical poems, abiding by the principle of "translating poesie into poesie", I firstly retain the original's metrical features and never misuse a translator's freedom to arbitrarily abandon the original's metrical features at the expense of damaging its poetic beauty. Also, I don't advocate unnaturally piling up rhymes at the cost of damaging meanings and twisting poetic structures. After all, going beyond the limit is as bad as falling short. Rhyme and rhythm are rooted in meaning or context, and as a significant part of poetic structure, they should not be sacrificed. They contribute to the overall poetic effect and will affect the whole body if ignored. Specifically speaking, "translating poesie into poesie" is in the condition that translators have realized the role of poetic form as a poem's base or template, at first fixing the translation's form as a poem. Translating a Chinese poem into an English blank verse or an English rhymed poem uneven in length does not conform to my aesthetic orientation. Though there is no compulsory limit for poetry translation, general translation techniques that are useful for specific performance and evaluation can be summarized from translation practice. For instance, in English, one foot generally consists of two syllables, and accordingly five feet equals ten syllables in English, which can tentatively match seven Chinese characters both in form and content. By analogy, I have set a set of rules below: translating a Chinese three-character line into a pentasyllabic line in English, a Chinese four-character line into a hexasyllabic line, a Chinese five-character line into an octosyllabic line, a Chinese six-character line into an enneasyllabic line, a Chinese seven-character line into a decasyllabic line, a Chinese eight-character line into a twelve-syllable line, and a

Chinese nine-character line into a fourteen-syllable line and so on.

In the second place, as rhymed poems account for the largest part of poems, when translating rhymed Chinese poems, the translations must be in rhyme, as the principle of "translating poesie into poesie, translating it as it is" entails "translating rhyme into rhyme". It is something that a translator should never make a concession to. Of course, a translator can decide which rhyme or which rhyming scheme to use. Since rhymes are something of analogy, except some unique poetic styles or subgenres, the rhyming schemes applied in a translation can be relatively flexible. The commonly used rhyming schemes in my translations include couplets (aa), alternate rhymes (abab) or interlacing rhymes (abcb). Most English poems use Iambus as the meter pattern along with auxiliaries such as Trochee, Anapaest and Dactyl, relevant to the requirement of meaning. A translation can do likewise. During the process, a translator should constantly focus on form-meaning tension, avoid the misuse of rhymes at the cost of damaging meaning, and ensure that the translated poem can possibly represent the original's style, emotion and imagery and then can achieve the validity of, and fidelity to, the original to the largest extent. Metrical patterns of English poetry, unlike those of Chinese metrical poems, are less strict. And the general principle is being harmonious in rhyme. A high-quality translation of a poem should be pithy, smooth and natural.

In the third place, apart from the representation of the original's poetic forms and metrical patterns, one more difficulty for translation is how to translate culture-loaded words. Chinese culture is an ancient civilization of great complexity, incomparable in profoundness and exclusively rich in dimension. It consists of diverse motifs such as plant images and art images, such as "wintersweets, orchids, bamboos and chrysanthemums", "zither, go, calligraphy, and painting", "Three Kings and Five Lords", and "Three Canons and Five Constants", all of which are outcomes of Chinese culture, and a single image can convey different meanings in different contexts and can be given a new content according to a certain language use. In the English translation of practice of Chinese ancient poetry, a responsible translator must never escape from interpreting these images and conveying their connotations in translation, for the reason that the purpose of translation is exactly to promote mutual understanding among all civilizations rather than a dialogue of the deaf. The use of culture-loaded words frequently manifests and shapes a poet's unique style, such as Pai Li's style of romanticism, Chü-e Pai's style of realism and Wei Wang's style of naturalism. Poetry translation also centers on the aesthetics of translating the taste. Simple literal translation is none but translation of words, not translation of literature. In this sense, excellent translations of poems should be as self-consistent as the original as well, and should mirror the original's literary style.

When faced with the occasions of culture default in the English translation of Chinese ancient poems, I choose the way of annotation to provide additional information outside the translated poems. However, in regard of translation, annotations belong to the type of paratext, namely, another text independent of the main body. For Chinese readers, background information of a Chinese ancient poem is a default value, and is not an essential part for the original though it affects Chinese readers' comprehension to some extent. Annotations in Chinese contexts can only reveal hidden knowledge some Chinese readers may need to know while reading, while for English readers, annotations in a translated text can be of great use and significance for them to comprehend the translation, which is an integral whole. Annotating is different from translating in the operational method. While providing annotations, a translator does not need to be imaginative, creative or sensitive, and instead needs to investigate and verify messages, to select those useful out of all and finally to summarize them into definitions. Meanwhile, a translator needs to refer to most recent archaeological findings to ensure that an annotation is able to contain complete and required historic and cultural elements with the most precise expressions. In turn, annotations can verify the degree of accuracy of translations, help translators to check and correct errors, and enhance the quality.

During the process of translation and annotation, translators must be concerned about culture-loaded words, lest some information be lost, distorted or redundant. As far as I can see, to ensure the fidelity to the original's information and readability of its translation, transliteration should be avoided as much as possible; if there is no better method than transliteration, translators should fully attend to westerners' reading habits, for example, I adopt the Wade-Giles romanization, for it has been popular with westerners and overseas Chinese. What is crucial is to avoid the hybridity of recodification, for example, the encoding of the hierarchy of Chinese culture is top-down while in English it is a bottom-up direction, just the opposite, for example, "Stonegate Vihara at Mt. Blue Field", which shows a bottom-up arrangement, is good English while "at Mt. Blue Field Stonegate Vihara" is absurd. Similarly, in "Pai Li", "Pai" is first name while "Li" is family name or surname, it is good English, while "Li Pai" violates the rule of English, just like the case we call Karl Marks "Marks Karl", so preposterous. So, "Pai Li" is the right address.

As for those salient and peculiar words in Chinese culture like Ching Wei, Hou E, Chuan Hsü and hsiuts'ai, considering that their cultural connotations will vanish in translations if transliteration is applied, I suggest that translators coin English words based on Chinese etymology and English word-formation, so as to reveal the original's word origin and introduce new eastern cultural connotations to the English world. This use of lexicon's intertextuality in cultural systems can assist English readers to deduce the signified of culture-loaded words from the translated context. For example, the word "xiu cai" or "hsiu ts'ai" makes no sense to English readers, while the recodification, like "showcharm" can trigger off similar associations, and as the target reader's cognitive environment is improved, he may have the same cognitive effect as source text readers. Through translation strategies mentioned above, a translator will be able to retain the original's allusions in the translated text to the largest extent, and provide annotations via footnotes to explain historical stories, myths, legends, and customs in the original and to delve into their connotations. So to speak, annotations play a positive role in achieving the goal of mutual understanding and compensating for the unintelligibility of cultural default brought about by the facsimiles of translation.

All in all, if a translator abides by the principle of "translating poesie into poesie, translating it as it is" and the principle of proximity while rendering Chinese ancient poetry into English, attempts to represent the original's poetic form and rhyming patterns, and provides annotations to assist translations of culture-loaded words, a translated poem can be concise and insightful, well-worded and refined, achieving the dialectical unity of beauty in form, meaning and musicality, just like the original. In this way, a translated poem can be approximate and equal to the original. Hence, in poetry translation, translations are likely to match and even exceed the original, and it depends on how a translator solves the explicability-unexplicability paradox and how he solves the riddle of Sphinx in translation.

Throughout the current translation studies and practices, it can be seen that most translators are still trapped in the static transformation of language codes at discourse level, due to the lack of a metaphysical metatheory, the ontology of translation and the ontology of language. Inevitably, their translations are unfaithful and distorted. Looking back at the course of translation of Chinese classics, translations at present have overshadowed the glory of Chinese civilization, split the oneness of the East and the West, failed to promote cultural exchanges and ironically turned out to be a barrier for cultural communication.

On the basis of a deep understanding of the ontology of translation and the ontology of language and taking substantial English translation of Chinese classics as solid evidences, I call for the innovation in translation methodology for finding a way out of the *status quo*. I suggest that translators start from the ontology of translation, synthetically apply etymology, syntax, semantics, philosophy and even theology in translation practice, and thus break through mechanical dualism. They are also expected to look upon translation as a dialectical system full of paradoxes from a holistic and holographic viewpoint. In this way, they may systematically reconcile contradictions like the translatability-untranslatability paradox; and they may pursue self-consistence of cultures as well as texts during the process of approximation and convergence in form and meaning. We look forward to the nirvana of translation theories and a refreshed look of translation of Chinese classics.

Thanks to the encouragement of the age, an age of the renaissance of traditional Chinese culture, we have access to the great treasures of knowledge. Along with bilingual studies of Chinese classics stepping into a new stage, we are experiencing the renewal of translation of Chinese classics. In this context, I have been committing myself to academic researches and translation practices for many years. I hope that the translated works of Wei Wang, Pai Li, Fu Tu and Chü-e Pai will give a true picture of what T'ang poetry is like, and that along with my other translated works of Chinese classics, these translations will keep on offering reliable resources for readers in China and overseas and will help Chinese culture to "go global" in a way.

Yanchun Chao
September 1, 2020
Shanghai University

目 录
Contents

1	**序言**	
	Introduction	
1	**译者自序**	
	Introduction by the Translator	
1	赋得古原草送别	
	Seeing a Friend Off by an Old Grassland	
2	望月有感	
	Perturbed When Looking at the Moon	
4	赠卖松者	
	To the Seller of Pine Saplings	
5	同李十一醉忆元九	
	Thinking of Chen Yüan While Drinking with Li Eleven	
6	望驿台	
	The Post Gazing Mound	
7	江楼月	
	The Moon over the Riverside Tower	
8	惜牡丹花	
	Sighing at the Peonies	
9	村夜	
	One Night in the Village	
10	欲与元八卜邻，先有是赠	
	To My New Neighbor Yüan Eight	
12	燕子楼三首	
	Swallow Tower, Three Poems	

15	花非花	
	Bloom, No Bloom	
16	初贬官过望秦岭	
	A Visit to Ch'in-Viewing Peak en Route to Exile	
17	琵琶行	
	A Pipa Player	
24	南浦别	
	Good-bye at South Shore	
25	大林寺桃花	
	Peach Blossoms in Greatwood Temple	
26	遗爱寺	
	Temple of Love	
27	问刘十九	
	Inviting Liu Nineteen	
28	夜雪	
	Snow at Night	
29	钟陵饯送	
	Farewell Feast at Bellridge	
30	李白墓	
	Pai Li's Tomb	
31	后宫词	
	A Concubine's Lament	
32	夜筝	
	Zither Playing at Night	
33	勤政楼西老柳	
	The Old Willow Tree West of the Administration Hall	
34	暮江吟	
	The River at Dusk	
35	寒闺怨	
	A Wife's Plaint in Autumn	
36	钱塘湖春行	
	A Spring Trip to Ch'ient'ang Lake	

38	春题湖上	
	An Inscription for the Lake in Spring	
39	西湖晚归回望孤山寺赠诸客	
	Looking Back at the Lone Hill on My Way Across West Lake	
41	杭州春望	
	Spring View in Hangchow	
42	别州民	
	Farewell to People of Hangchow	
43	白云泉	
	White Cloud Fountain	
44	秋雨夜眠	
	Sleeping on a Rainy Autumn Night	
45	与梦得沽酒闲饮且约后期	
	Drinking at Leisure Together with Dream Gained and Making an Appointment to Meet Again	
46	览卢子蒙侍御旧诗，多与微之唱和，感今伤昔，因赠子蒙，题于卷后	
	On Reading Tsumeng Lu's Old Poems Written in the Same Rhyming Scheme with Chen Yüan's, Usually in Response to Weitsu, So Moved, I Write This, Dedicated to Tsumeng, Inscribed at the End of the Chapter	
48	红鹦鹉	
	The Red Parrot	
49	昼卧	
	Lying in Bed at Daytime	
50	病中五绝（其五）	
	In Illness (No. 5)	
51	杨柳枝词	
	Song of Willow Twigs	
52	忆江南	
	Dreaming of South	
53	长相思	
	Long Longing	
54	长恨歌	
	Lasting Grief	

64	池上	
	On the Pool	
65	喜雨	
	A Blessing Rain	
67	村居苦寒	
	Bitter Winter in the Village	
69	宿紫阁山北村	
	A Night at North Village in Mt. Purple Tower	
71	观刈麦	
	Watching the Wheat Reapers	
74	大水	
	The Flood	
76	新制布裘	
	My New Gown	
78	纳粟	
	Collecting Grain Tax	
80	采地黄者	
	The Rehmannia Gatherer	
82	赠友诗五首（选二）	
	To My Friend (Two out of Five)	
87	开龙门八节石滩二首	
	Dredging Eight Stone Rapids at Dragongate, Two Poems	
90	折剑头	
	A Broken Sword	
92	放鹰	
	Letting Out the Falcon	
95	紫藤	
	Wisteria	
98	悲哉行	
	O Sad	
101	杏园中枣树	
	The Date Tree in the Apricot Orchard	

104	梦仙
	Dreaming of Being an Immortal
108	凶宅
	The Haunted Estate
113	有木诗八首
	Eight Poems of Plants
129	寓意诗五首
	Five Allegorical Poems
139	秦中吟十首（选三）
	Chants in Long Peace (Three Poems Out of Ten)
139	议婚
	Marriage
142	重赋
	Heavy Tax
145	买花
	Buying Flowers
147	续古诗十首
	Ten Old Poems
165	龙昌寺荷池
	The Lotus Pool at Dragonrise Temple
166	食饱
	Well Fed
167	夜雨
	Night Rain
169	邯郸冬至夜思家
	Thinking of Home on the Night of Winter Solstice in Hantan
171	赠内
	To My Wife
174	寄内
	A Letter for My Wife
175	赠内
	To My Wife

176	寄江南兄弟	
	A Letter to My Brothers in the South	
178	寄行简	
	To Hsingchien, My Brother	
180	闻龟儿咏诗	
	On Hearing Tortoise Chanting a Poem	
181	哭崔儿	
	Mourning Ts'ui, My Son	
182	感情	
	Love of the Shoes	
184	开元九诗书卷	
	Opening Chen Yüan's Works	
185	蓝桥驿见元九诗	
	Reading Chen Yüan's Poem at Blue Bridge Post	
186	寄生衣与微之，因题封上	
	Sending Summer Clothes to Weichih, Written on the Wrap	
187	舟中读元九诗	
	Reading Chen Yüan's Poems on a Boat	
188	初与元九别后忽梦见之及寤而书适至兼寄桐花诗，怅然感怀，因以此寄	
	After Parting from Chen Yüan, I Dreamed of Him; when I Awoke, His Letter and Verse of *Chinese Scholar Tree Flower* Arrived. Therefore, So Perturbed, I Wrote This.	
192	商山路驿桐树，昔与微之前后题名处	
	Halting at a Phoenix Tree on the Way by Mt. Shang; Chen Yüan and I Both Left Our Inscriptions Here	
193	梦与李七、庚三十三同访元九	
	My Dream of Visiting Chen Yüan with Li Seven and Yü Thirty-Three	
196	赠梦得	
	To Yühsi Liu	
198	久不见韩侍郎，戏题四韵以寄之	
	I Haven't Seen Vice Premier for Long, So I Send Him Four Couplets for Fun	

199	以镜赠别	
	A Mirror as a Parting Present	
201	访陶公旧宅	
	A Visit to Poolbright T'ao's Old House	
205	江南遇天宝乐叟	
	Coming Across an Old Musician in the South in the Heaven-Blessed Reign	
209	东楼招客夜饮	
	Inviting Guests to a Drink on East Tower	
210	故衫	
	My Old Gown	
211	读李杜诗集因题卷后	
	Reading Li and Tu's Collection of Poems, Hence My Inscription on the Back Cover	
213	听夜筝有感	
	Perturbed at the Cheng at Night	
214	放言五首(选三)	
	Bold Words, Five Poems (Three out of Five)	
217	登商山最高顶	
	Climbing to the Apex of Mt. Shang	
219	秋蝶	
	An Autumn Butterfly	
221	别草堂三绝句	
	Farewell to Thatched Cottage, Three Quatrains	
224	新乐府五十首(选二十二)	
	New Conservertoire, Fifty Poems (Twenty-two out of Fifty)	
224	海漫漫	
	The Surging Vast Sea	
227	上阳白发人	
	The White-Haired Uppershine Belle	
231	胡旋女	
	O Hun Dancing Girl	

234	太行路	
	The Way to Mt. Great Go	
237	道州民	
	The Dwarfs of Taochow	
239	缚戎人	
	Jung Prisoners of War	
244	骊宫高	
	Black Steed Palace	
247	两朱阁	
	Two Red Towers	
249	涧底松	
	Pines in the Dale	
251	牡丹芳	
	O Peony So Fine	
256	红线毯	
	The Red Silk Carpet	
259	杜陵叟	
	The Old Man of Birchleaf Hill	
261	缭绫	
	Twine Silk	
264	卖炭翁	
	The Charcoal Gray Hair	
266	官牛	
	The Official Ox	
268	紫毫笔	
	The Purple Hair Brush	
271	隋堤柳	
	Sui Dyke Willows Gray	
275	古冢狐	
	The Ancient Tomb Fox	
277	黑潭龙	
	The Black Pool Dragon	

279	天可度	
	We Can Gauge the Earth	
281	秦吉了	
	The Grackle	
284	采诗官	
	The Folk Song Scribe	

287 **译者简介**
About the Translator

赋得古原草送别

离离原上草，
一岁一枯荣，
野火烧不尽，
春风吹又生。
远芳侵古道，
晴翠接荒城，
又送王孙去，
萋萋满别情。

Seeing a Friend Off by an Old Grassland

Rolling, rolling, the grassland's grass
Blooms or dries as time turns to pass.
A wild fire can't all of it burn;
A spring wind heralds its return.
The fragrance does the old road drown;
The green spreads to the dreary town.
Now I see you off once again,
Sad, sad, the grass is filled with pain.

* The poem was composed in A.D. 787, when the poet was 16 years old.
* wild fire: a fire in the wild, as is used as a metaphor in this poem.

望 月 有 感

自河南经乱,关内阻饥,兄弟离散,各在一处。因望月有感,聊书所怀,寄上浮梁大兄,於潜七兄,乌江十五兄,兼示符离及下邽弟妹。

时难年荒世业空,
弟兄羁旅各西东。
田园寥落干戈后,
骨肉流离道路中。
吊影分为千里雁,
辞根散作九秋蓬。
共看明月应垂泪,
一夜乡心五处同。

Perturbed When Looking at the Moon

Since the tumult of Honan, there has been starvation and hindrance and my siblings have been scattered. I write this poem for them to express myself by the light of the moon, and thereafter send it to my eldest brother in Fuliang, elder brother Seven in Yuchien, elder brother Fifteen in Wuchiang and shown to younger siblings in Fuli and Hsiakui.

Hard times with famine and ruins, so hard pressed;
My brothers all go their way, east or west.
Warfare has caused fields and parks to lie waste;
Families scattered flee their land in haste.
We're stray wild geese that to their shadows cheep,
And scattered thistledown in autumn deep.

We all shed tears while viewing the moon bright;
In five places, we have the same heart all night.

* Honan: Honan See, covering the major part of today's Honan Province, some part of Shantung, Chiangsu, and Anhui Province. See, tao if transliterated, is the first administrative unit, mainly in charge of inspection and jurisdiction. The T'ang Empire was divided into 10 sees, 358 prefectures and 1,551 counties in Emperor Firstsire's reign.
* Fuliang: today's Chingtechen, Chianghsi Province.
* Yuchien: today's Lin'an County, Chechiang Province.
* Wuchiang: today's Ho County, Anhui Province.
* Fuli: today's Fuli, Suchow, Anhui Province, Chü-e Pai's hometown.
* wild goose: an undomesticated goose that is caring and responsible, taken as a symbol of benevolence, righteousness, good manner, wisdom, and faith in Chinese culture.
* thistledown: the pappus of a thistle, a kind of vigorous prickly plant with cylindrical or globular heads of tubular purple flowers, an important image in Chinese literature, a metaphor for vagrants or strayers.

赠 卖 松 者

一束苍苍色,
知从涧底来。
斸掘经几日,
枝叶满尘埃。
不买非他意,
城中无地栽。

To the Seller of Pine Saplings

Lo, a bundle of emerald green
Comes from the deep dale I ween.
Dug up for only several days,
All dust on the leaves and sprays.
It's not that I will not them buy;
I can't plant downtown far or nigh.

* a bundle of emerald green: a metonymy for pine saplings.

同李十一醉忆元九

花时同醉破春愁，
醉折花枝当酒筹。
忽忆故人天际去，
计程今日到梁州。

Thinking of Chen Yüan While Drinking with Li Eleven

We drink amid flowers in spring to kill time;
I pluck flower twigs as chips to drink and rhyme.
Ho, my friend's gone far, far away;
I reckon, he'll be in Liangchow today.

* Chen Yüan: Chen Yüan (A.D. 779 – A.D. 831), a famous T'ang poet, Pai's closest friend, the two forming a dyad in the history of Chinese Literature.
* Liangchow: in today's Mid Han (Hanchung), Sha'anhsi Province.

望 驿 台

靖安宅里当窗柳，
望驿台前扑地花。
两处春光同日尽，
居人思客客思家。

The Post Gazing Mound

The willow at home does the window sway;
Flowers fall all over the Post Gazing Mound.
Spring ends in two places on the same day;
She thinks of you, you think of her, profound.

* willow: any of a large genus of shrubs and trees related to the poplars, having generally smooth branches, and often long, slender, pliant, and sometimes pendent branchlets, a symbol of farewell or nostalgia in Chinese culture. The best image of a weeping willow in Chinese literature is in *Vetch We Pick*, a verse in *The Book of Songs*, which is like this: When we left long ago, / The willows waved adieu. / Now back to our home town, / We meet snow falling down.
* the Post Gazing Mound: in today's Kuangyüan, Ssuch'uan Province.

江　楼　月

嘉陵江曲曲江池，
明月虽同人别离。
一宵光景潜相忆，
两地阴晴远不知。
谁料江边怀我夜，
正当池畔望君时。
今朝同吾方共悔，
不解多情先寄诗。

The Moon over the Riverside Tower

The Fineridge bends and the Bent also bends;
The moon is the same, we're at different ends.
All night you pine for me; for you I pine.
I don't know if we've the same rain or shine.
Who knows when riverside for me you yearn,
Waterside here I miss you with concern?
Today your verse arrived, I regret now
Why didn't I send you mine earlier, how?

* the Fineridge: an upper branch of the Long River, so named because it flows through the Fineridge Valley northeast of Phoenix County of today's Sha'anhsi Province.
* the Bent River: Ch'uchiang if transliterated, a royal park of T'ang, located in the southeast of Long Peace, the capital.

惜牡丹花

惆怅阶前红牡丹，
晚来唯有两枝残。
明朝风起应吹尽，
夜惜衰红把火看。

Sighing at the Peonies

At the step-by peonies so red I sigh;
At dusk but two of them are left to dry.
Tomorrow they will be blown to expire;
At night I gaze at them holding a fire.

* peony: any of a genus of perennial, often double-flowered, plants of the peony family, with large pink, yellow, red, or white showy flowers, cultivated as early as the Sui dynasty in China, became popular in the T'ang dynasty and well-known in the Sung dynasty. The best peonies are those cultivated in Loshine.

村　夜

霜草苍苍虫切切，
村南村北行人绝。
独出前门望野田，
月明荞麦花如雪。

One Night in the Village

Green, green frosty grass, chirp, chirp insects cry;
North and south of the burg, none's on the go.
Now outdoors, down the field I cast an eye;
The moonlit buckwheat blossoms look like snow.

* buckwheat: any of several plants of the buckwheat family, grown for their black, triangular grains.

欲与元八卜邻,先有是赠

平生心迹最相亲,
欲隐墙东不为身。
明月好同三径夜,
绿杨宜作两家春。
每因暂出犹思伴,
岂得安居不择邻?
可独终身数相见,
子孙长作隔墙人。

To My New Neighbor Yüan Eight

Let's be close friends mind to mind, heart to heart;
I'll share your wall, not for good life to start.
The moon shines so bright for both you and me;
The green willows bring us a shade for free.
Even on short tours we need have a friend;
When settled, on neighbors we should depend.
All our life each other we could oft see;
I pray our offspring could good neighbors be.

* the moon: an important image in Chinese literature or culture as it can give rise to many associations such as solitude and nostalgia on the one hand, and purity, brightness and happy reunions on the other. Philosophically, it is the very germ or source of Shade, and the sun is its Shine counterpart. The moon is celebrated with mooncakes in China on Mid-autumn Day when the moon is at its full glory.
* willow: any of a large genus (*Salix*) of shrubs and trees related to the poplars, having generally smooth branches, and often long, slender, pliant, and sometimes pendent

branchlets, a symbol of farewell or nostalgia in Chinese culture. The best image is in *Vetch We Pick*, a verse in *The Book of Songs*, which is like this: When we left long ago, / The willows waved adieu. / Now back to our home town, / We meet snow falling down.

燕子楼三首
Swallow Tower, Three Poems

其 一

满窗明月满帘霜，
被冷灯残拂卧床。
燕子楼中霜月夜，
秋来只为一人长。

No. 1

The window's pale with frost neath Luna bright;
Quilt cold, the lamplight so weak strokes my bed.
Swallow Tower stands still on the frosty night
The autumn's long for me, for me instead.

---

* Luna: the moon, an important image in Chinese literature or culture as it can give rise to many associations such as solitude and nostalgia on the one hand, and purity, brightness and happy reunions on the other. What is "moon" in Chinese has at least two hundred names, like Jade Mound (yaot'ai), Fair Lady (ch'anchüan), Jade Hare (yüt'u), White Hare (pait'u), Silver Hare (yint'u), Ice Hare (pingt'u), Gold Hare (chint'u), Hare Gleam (t'uhui), Laurel Soul (Kuip'o) and so on.

* Swallow Tower: one of the five most famous towers in Hsuchow, so named because it looks like a flying swallow. It was built by Yin Chang (? – A.D. 806), Governor of Martial Peace, for his concubine, a famous poetess of the T'ang dynasty.

其 二

钿晕罗衫色似烟，
几回欲著即潸然。
自从不舞霓裳曲，
叠在空箱十一年。

No. 2

Silken robes and golden flowers will all decay;
She would put it on, but there fall her tears.
For long she has not danced *Rainbow Dress Lay*;
Her dress has lain in the chest for ten years.

* *Rainbow Dress*: also called *Rainbow Plumage Dance* — a kind of court dance in the T'ang dynasty, to the accompaniment of a tune called Rainbow Plumage, which was believed to have been composed by Emperor Deepsire of T'ang.

其 三

今春有客洛阳回，
曾到尚书墓上来。
见说白杨堪作柱，
争教红粉不成灰？

No. 3

This spring back from Loshine there comes a friend;
To the minister's graveyard he does wend.
A poplar could be a beam, as is said;
Her face would be ash though once beaming red.

* Loshine: Loyang if transliterated, one of the four ancient capitals in China, along with Long Peace (Hsi'an), Gold Hill (Nanking) and Peking, and it was the second largest city and the eastern capital of the T'ang dynasty, with a population of 800,000. It was first built from 1735 B.C. to 1540 B.C. in the Hsia dynasty as its political center, and in 1046 B.C. Prince of Chough built two cities here in order to control Chough's east territory. In 770 B.C. King Peace of Chough moved to this place when Warmer (Haoching), Chough's capital, was captured by Hounds (Ch'üanjung), hence the Eastern Chough dynasty. Since its founding, Loshine has been a capital for thirteen dynasties.
* poplar: any of a genus (*Populus*) of dioecious trees and bushes of the willow family, widely distributed in the northern hemisphere.

花 非 花

花非花，
雾非雾，
夜半来，
天明去。
来如春梦几多时？
去似朝云无觅处。

Bloom, No Bloom

Bloom, no bloom;
Brume, no brume.
Night, it's on;
Morn, it's run.
Like a spring dream, going, gone;
Like a morn cloud, lost anon.

* morn cloud: or dawn cloud, an allusion to the legend of Goddess of Mt. Witch. Goddess of Mt. Witch is a good-looking fairy who shapes herself as clouds at dawn and turns to rain at dusk. In the myths, King Huai of Ch'u once met her and had an intercourse overnight in his dream. The story was recorded by Jade Sung, a student of Yüan Ch'ü.

初贬官过望秦岭

草草辞家忧后事，
迟迟去国问前途。
望秦岭上回头立，
无限秋风吹白须。

A Visit to Ch'in-Viewing Peak en Route to Exile

Leaving in haste, I care things after hand;
Not knowing what will be, I linger there.
Now on Ch'in-Viewing Peak homeward I stand,
Let the endless autumn breeze blow my hair.

* Ch'in-Viewing Peak: Mt. Ch'in's Ridge at Shangchow (under Shanhsi Province today).

琵琶行

浔阳江头夜送客,
枫叶荻花秋索索。
主人下马客在船,
举酒欲饮无管弦。
醉不成欢惨将别,
别时茫茫江浸月。
忽闻水上琵琶声,
主人忘归客不发。
寻声暗问弹者谁?
琵琶声停欲语迟。
移船相近邀相见,
添酒回灯重开宴。
千呼万唤始出来,
犹抱琵琶半遮面。
转轴拨弦三两声,
未成曲调先有情。
弦弦掩抑声声思,
似诉平生不得意。
低眉信手续续弹,
说尽心中无限事。
轻拢慢捻抹复挑,
初为霓裳后六幺。
大弦嘈嘈如急雨,
小弦切切如私语。
嘈嘈切切错杂弹,
大珠小珠落玉盘。
间关莺语花底滑,

幽咽泉流冰下难。
冰泉冷涩弦凝绝,
凝绝不通声暂歇。
别有幽愁暗恨生,
此时无声胜有声。
银瓶乍破水浆迸,
铁骑突出刀枪鸣。
曲终收拨当心画,
四弦一声如裂帛。
东船西舫悄无言,
唯见江心秋月白。
沉吟放拨插弦中,
整顿衣裳起敛容。
自言本是京城女,
家在虾蟆陵下住。
十三学得琵琶成,
名属教坊第一部。
曲罢曾教善才服,
妆成每被秋娘妒。
五陵年少争缠头,
一曲红绡不知数。
钿头银篦击节碎,
血色罗裙翻酒污。
今年欢笑复明年,
秋月春风等闲度。
弟走从军阿姨死,
暮去朝来颜色故。
门前冷落鞍马稀,
老大嫁作商人妇。
商人重利轻别离,
前月浮梁买茶去。

去来江口守空船,
绕船月明江水寒。
夜深忽梦少年事,
梦啼妆泪红阑干。
我闻琵琶已叹息,
又闻此语重唧唧。
同是天涯沦落人,
相逢何必曾相识!
我从去年辞帝京,
谪居卧病浔阳城。
浔阳地僻无音乐,
终岁不闻丝竹声。
住近湓江地低湿,
黄芦苦竹绕宅生。
其间旦暮闻何物?
杜鹃啼血猿哀鸣。
春江花朝秋月夜,
往往取酒还独倾。
岂无山歌与村笛?
呕哑嘲哳难为听。
今夜闻君琵琶语,
如听仙乐耳暂明。
莫辞更坐弹一曲,
为君翻作《琵琶行》。
感我此言良久立,
却坐促弦弦转急。
凄凄不似向前声,
满座重闻皆掩泣。
座中泣下谁最多?
江州司马青衫湿。

A Pipa Player

Tonight ashore I bid my friend good-bye;
Maples and reeds rustle — the rustles sigh.
My friend and I dismount and get aboard;
There is no pipe or strings for spirit poured
So drunk without cheer, I'll be leaving soon;
Just now the river tides up to the moon.
Sudd'nly o'er the stream floats a pipa sound;
I forget to go, and my friend's there bound.
Following the tune, the player I will seek.
Pipa stopped; she hesitates, hard to speak.
We move our boat near, to see her we're fain,
Lamp relit, more wine filled, we'll drink again.
She shows up at many a call and shout,
Her face half behind the pipa, half out.
She turns the pluck and plucks the strings to test;
Before a tune is played, she's self-expressed.
The strings she plucks pluck up her depressed thought
For all life, no ideal life has she got.
Her brows lowered, she plays round after round;
She pours out her emotions without bound.
She lightly plucks, slowly twirls and twangs loud,
A-playing *Green Waist* after *Rainbow Cloud*.
The thick strings thrum loudly, rash like a rain;
The thin strings swing softly, sweet like a cane.
Loud notes, soft notes are alternately played;
Big pearls, small pearls drop on a plate of jade.
Orioles chirp beneath flowers twice or thrice,

A sobbing stream flows hindered under ice.
Cold, the strings tightened and the tune depressed,
As sobs check her voice, it stops for a rest.
All the same, her well concealed grief bursts out;
Right now, silence speaks louder than a shout.
A silver pot breaks and liquid does splash;
A horse charges, and halberds and spears clash.
She waves her pluck upward as the tune ends;
The four strings rebound as if a silk rends.
All silence aboard this yacht or that boat,
Only an autumn moon downstream afloat.
She slides the pluck through the strings apposed,
Smooths out her dress and rises, so composed.
She comes from the capital, she does tell;
The foot of Mt. Toad is where she did dwell.
At thirteen she had mastered pipa play,
And come out as a best player of the day.
For her great skill she was acknowledged well;
And her charm was envied by any belle.
The gallant youngsters vied to win her smiles;
One tune played, of silk she got piles and piles.
Beating time, I let silver comb and pin clink,
And spilt-out wine oft stained my skirt so pink.
From year to year I did laugh as I please,
Living with the autumn moon and spring breeze.
Then brother mine went to war, 'nd died my maid;
Dusk passed, dawn came, and my beauty did fade.
Fewer and fewer cabs and steeds came to my door;
I married a merchant when young no more.
The merchant cared for gold more than for me;
Last month he went to Fuliang to buy tea.

He left, letting me keep to the void boat;
The moon lit the river cold, where I did float.
The night so deep, I dreamt of my past years;
I often wept o'er my rouge and dried tears.
Having heard her play I heaved a long sigh;
Now at her tale, hardly could I reply.
We're both vagrants at the end of the sky;
Need we have been friends, far away or nigh?
I bade bye to the capital last year;
Debased and diseased in the city here.
Sun-gain has no music, no music stirred;
All year round no pipes or strings can be heard.
I live near the river humid and cold,
Yellow reeds and bitter bamboo in mould.
From dawn to dusk what the hell can you hear?
Cuckoo's cries and gibbon's shrieks rasp your ear.
Spring river, flower morning and autumn moon,
All alone, to my lonely wine I croon!
Aren't there mountain songs and folk pipes to hear?
The voice hoarse and sound husky pain the ear.
I hark to your pipa well played tonight,
As though your sweet tune makes my hearing bright.
Don't decline, sit down again and do play;
I'll write *The Pipa* for you right away.
Moved by my request he stands there for long,
And then seated she plucks the strings, strung, strung.
Sad, sad, unlike the song performed before,
All those seated cry, having heard once more.
Who of the audience weeps the most, so keen?
Bankshine's commander has soaked his shirt green.

* pipa: a plucked string instrument made of wood or bamboo, as large as a cello, widely used in Asia.
* maple: any of a large genus (*Acer*) of deciduous trees of the north temperate zone, with opposite leaves that turn red in autumn and a fruit of two joined samaras, a symbol of cordial love and good luck because of its bright fiery color.
* reed: the slender, frequently jointed stem of certain tall grasses growing in wet places or in grasses themselves. A frosted reed is an image of the white hair of one getting old or suffering a mishap.
* *Green Waist*: one of the famous tunes in the T'ang dynasty.
* pearl: a lustrous, calcareous concretion deposited in layers around a central nucleus in the shells of various mollusks, and largely used as a gem, regarded as a treasure or given as a gift to represent love and friendship.
* *Rainbow Cloud*: referring to *Rainbow Cloud* dance or plumage dance, a kind of court dance in the T'ang dynasty, to the accompaniment of a tune called *Rainbow Plumage*, which was believed to have been composed by Emperor Deepsire of T'ang.
* Mt. Toad: a famous park near the River Bent southeast of Long Peace.
* silk: the fine, soft, shiny fiber produced by silk worms to form their cocoons, and the thread or fabric made from this fibre is used as material for clothing. And it can be any clothing made of silk.
* Fuliang: today's Chingtechen, Chianghsi Province.
* Bankshine, formally called Riverton, most part of today's Chianghsi Province and some part of Chechiang Province. One of the prefectures of the T'ang Empire.

南 浦 别

南浦凄凄别,
西风袅袅秋。
一看肠一断,
好去莫回头。

Good-bye at South Shore

At South Shore we bid painful bye;
West wind to the autumn does blow.
A broken heart, and a sad sigh;
Do not turn back, ahead you go.

* South Shore: south of a river, a metonymy for a place where one bids farewell.

大林寺桃花

人间四月芳菲尽,
山寺桃花始盛开。
长恨春归无觅处,
不知转入此中来。

Peach Blossoms in Greatwood Temple

As the world's April blossoms lose their grace,
In the hill fane peach flowers begin to blow.
All hate that spring has gone off without trace;
It has turned to prosper here you don't know.

* Greatwood Temple: one of the three most famous temples on Mt. Lodge, the other two being Westwood Temple and Eastwood Temple.

遗 爱 寺

弄石临溪坐，
寻花绕寺行。
时时闻鸟语，
处处是泉声。

Temple of Love

To sit streamside, the stone I sweep,
And go round the fane for flowers fair.
From time to time you hear birds cheep,
And fountains gurgle everywhere.

* Temple of Love: a temple under the peak of Censer on Mt. Lodge.

问 刘 十 九

绿蚁新醅酒，
红泥小火炉。
晚来天欲雪，
能饮一杯无？

Inviting Liu Nineteen

Green ants afloat on the new brew,
The red clay stove is flaming up.
Now it's late, threatening snow;
Will you come in to drink a cup?

* green ants: foams or dross of newly brewed liquor, floating on the surface and looking like green ants.

夜　雪

已讶衾枕冷，
复见窗户明。
夜深知雪重，
时闻折竹声。

Snow at Night

My pillow feels cold I'm surprised
And I see window mine aglow
Snow's heavy I'm by night apprised
You oft hear the snap of bamboo.

* bamboo: a tall, tree-like or shrubby grass in tropical and semi-tropical regions, a symbol of integrity and altitude, one of the four most important images in Chinese literature, which are wintersweet, orchid, bamboo, and chrysanthemum.

钟 陵 饯 送

翠幕红筵高在云，
歌钟一曲万家闻。
路人指点滕王阁，
看送忠州白使君。

Farewell Feast at Bellridge

Green tents and red banquets point to the sky;
Songs and bells ten thousand houses can hear.
"Behold, Prince T'eng's Tower", says a passer-by;
The prefect hosts a farewell banquet here.

* Bellridge: a county established in the Sui dynasty, now Southboom (Nanch'ang), capital of today's Chianghsi Province.
* Prince T'eng: Emperor Grandsire's younger brother Yüanying Li (A.D. 628 – A.D. 684), famous for his revelry.

李 白 墓

采石江边李白坟，
绕田无限草连云。
可怜荒垄穷泉骨，
曾有惊天动地文。
但是诗人多薄命，
就中沦落不过君。

Pai Li's Tomb

Beside the Stonemill Stream lies Pai Li's tomb;
The grass around the field spreads to the skies.
His bones are buried here, enwrapped in gloom,
Although his songs take the world to surprise.
There're few poets who live long, very few,
But none has come down, as wretched as you.

* the Stonemill Stream: a stream near the Stonemill Protrusion, an important ferry in Ancient China.
* Pai Li's tomb: at the foot of the Green Hill in present-day Tangt'u, Anhui Province. According to one of Pai Li's granddaughters, Pai Li had expressed his desire of making the Green Hill at a short distance southeast of Great Peace (Taiping-fu) as his last resting place, so his tomb was moved from Mt. Dragon to the north side of the Green Hill in A.D. 818.

后　宫　词

泪湿罗巾梦不成，
夜深前殿按歌声。
红颜未老恩先断，
斜倚熏笼坐到明。

A Concubine's Lament

Scarf wet with tears, I couldn't sleep at all
But sing at night inside the frontal hall.
His love no more, tho' I'm far from old age;
Till morn I lean against the incense cage.

* incense cage: a cage for incense burning to perfume a bedroom, used in ancient China, especially in a harem.

夜　筝

紫袖红弦明月中，
自弹自感暗低容。
弦凝指咽声停处，
别有深情一万重。

Zither Playing at Night

The moon sees her violet sleeves and red strings;
She plucks, sighs and then lowers her moonlit face.
Her pluck halts, while she sobs and mutely sings,
There move ten thousand layers of love and grace.

* zither: a simple form of a stringed instrument, having a flat sounding board and from thirty to forty strings that are played by plucking with a plectrum. Zither, together with chess, calligraphy and painting are four skills that a traditional litterateur is expected to master.
* the moon: the satellite of the earth, a representative of shade or feminity of things, alluding to the solitude of the belle in this poem.

勤政楼西老柳

半朽临风树，
多情立马人。
开元一株柳，
长庆二年春。

The Old Willow Tree West of the Administration Hall

The breeze sways a half-rotten tree;
Astride my horse, calmed I can't be
It's witnessed years called All Begun;
Now's the second spring of Blessed One.

* the Administration Hall: in Rise of Bliss Palace, built in A.D. 720 and rebuilt in A.D. 819,
* All Begun: All Begun (A.D. 713 - A.D. 741), the reign title of Emperor Deepsire of T'ang. Allbegun is the most flourishing and powerful period of the T'ang Empire.
* Blessed One: Blessed One (Ch'angching if transliterated) (A.D. 821 - A.D. 824), the reign title of Emperor Solemn, Heng Li.

暮 江 吟

一道残阳铺水中，
半江瑟瑟半江红。
可怜九月初三夜，
露似真珠月似弓。

The River at Dusk

A fading streak of sunray's upstream spread;
The river's half emerald, and half red.
The third night of the ninth moon, oh you know,
The dew's like a pearl and the moon a bow.

* the moon: the satellite of the earth, a representative of shade or feminity of things, alluding to the belle in this poem. In a universe animated by the interaction of Shade and Shine energies, the moon is Shade visible, the very germ or source of Shade, and the sun is its Shine counterpart. It is the goddess of the moon and of months in Roman mythology, and in Chinese culture the imperial concubine of Lord Alarm (2480 B.C.-2345 B.C.), one of five mythical emperors in prehistorical China. The moon is celebrated with mooncakes by Chinese all over the world on Mid-autumn Day when the moon is at its full glory.
* pearl: a lustrous, calcareous concretion deposited in layers around a central nucleus in the shells of various mollusks, and largely used as a gem, a symbol of love or friendship in Chinese culture.

寒 闺 怨

寒月沉沉洞房静，
真珠帘外梧桐影。
秋霜欲下手先知，
灯底裁缝剪刀冷。

A Wife's Plaint in Autumn

The cool moon looks down over her bower still,
Outside the pearly screen moves a plane shade.
Autumn frost's falling her hand feels the chill;
Beneath her lamp cold scissors are there laid.

* the cool moon: an image of solitude in Chinese Literature.
* plane: plane tree, any of a genus of the plane-tree family having maple-like leaves, spherical dry fruits and bark that sheds in large patches.

钱塘湖春行

孤山寺北贾亭西,
水面初平云脚低。
几处早莺争暖树,
谁家新燕啄春泥。
乱花渐欲迷人眼,
浅草才能没马蹄。
最爱湖东行不足,
绿杨阴里白沙堤。

A Spring Trip to Ch'ient'ang Lake

North of Lone Hill Fane and west of Chia's Kiosk,
The lake falls serene with clouds hanging low.
A few orioles scramble for the warm tree;
Some swallows peck spring mud; where will they go?
The riot of flowers sway to dazzle the eye;
The grass sways shallow, just horse-hoof deep.
A stroll east of the lake does one beguile;
The willows with their green Whitesand Dyke sweep.

* Ch'ient'ang Lake: West Lake, west of Hangchow proper, one of the most famous attractions in China, with a rich historic legacy, like Su's Dyke, White Dyke, the Lone Hill, Petite's Tomb, Leifeng Pagoda and so on.
* Lone Hill Fane: a temple on the Lone Hill which is between Rear Lake and Outer Lake, two of the five lakes consisting of West Lake.
* Chia's Kiosk: a pavilion built by Ch'uan Chia (? – A.D. 805), mayor of Hangchow.
* oriole: golden oriole, one of the family of passerine birds, which looks bright yellow

with contrasting black wings and sings beautiful songs.
* swallow: a passerine black bird, with short broad, depressed bill, long pointed wings, and forked tail, noted for fleeting flight and migratory habits. In Chinese culture, swallows are welcome to live with a family with their nests on a beam.
* willow: any of a large genus of shrubs and trees related to the poplars, having generally smooth branches, and often long, slender, pliant, and sometimes pendent branchlets, a symbol of farewell, longing or nostalgia in Chinese culture.
* Whitesand Dyke: one of the dykes of West Lake.

春 题 湖 上

湖上春来似画图,
乱峰围绕水平铺。
松排山面千重翠,
月点波心一颗珠。
碧毯线头抽早稻,
青罗裙带展新蒲。
未能抛得杭州去,
一半勾留是此湖。

An Inscription for the Lake in Spring

When spring comes on, the lake's a picture true!
Rugged peaks surround water smooth and blue.
Hills upon hills the pines aligned look green,
The moon adores the waves with pearly sheen.
Green-carpet-like, the paddy fields show rice ears;
From the new bulrush a silk sash appears.
From Hangchow here how can I stride away,
The lake would fain keep me here in a way.

* the lake: referring to West Lake, one of the most famous lakes in China, boasting natural and historical attractions.
* pine: a cone-bearing tree having needle-shaped evergreen leaves growing in clusters, a symbol of longevity and rectitude in Chinese culture.
* Hangchow: the capital of today's Chechiang Province. The poet was its prefect from A.D. 822, the second year of Blessed One, to A.D. 824, the fourth year of Blessed One.

西湖晚归回望孤山寺赠诸客

柳湖松岛莲花寺,
晚动归桡出道场。
卢橘子低山雨重,
棕榈叶战水风凉。
烟波澹荡摇空碧,
楼殿参差倚夕阳。
到岸请君回首望,
蓬莱宫在海中央。

Looking Back at the Lone Hill on My Way Across West Lake

Lotus Temple, Pine Isle and Willow Lake,
Pilgrims come out at dusk a boat to take.
Loquats on trees in a rain from the hill,
Palm leaves wet with water and looking chill.
The misty ripples blending with the blue,
The afterglow touching the towers with hue.
When coming ashore, do turn around please:
The Fairy Isles are in the midst of the seas.

* West Lake: west of Hangchow proper, one of the most famous attractions in China, with a rich historic legacy, like Su's Dyke, White Dyke, the Lone Hill, Petite's Tomb, Leifeng Pagoda and so on.
* Lotus Temple: referring to Lone Hill Fane.
* Pine Isle: referring to the Lone Hill.
* Willow Lake: referring to West Lake, so called because of the willows on the bank.

* loquat: the yellow, small, edible, plum-like fruit of the loquat tree, a small evergreen tree of the rose family, native to China and Japan.
* palm: any of an order of tropical and subtropical monocotyledonous trees or shrubs, having a woody, usually unbranched, trunk, and large, evergreen or fan-shaped leaves growing in a bunch at the top.
* Fairy Isles: also known as Mt. Fairyland or Fairyland, three fairy isles held up by giant turtles in East Sea, a dwelling place of immortals and exalted spirits, regarded as today's P'englai Isles governed by Shantung Province.

杭 州 春 望

望海楼明照曙霞，
护江堤白踏晴沙。
涛声夜入伍员庙，
柳色春藏苏小家。
红袖织绫夸柿蒂，
青旗沽酒趁梨花。
谁开湖寺西南路？
草绿裙腰一道斜。

Spring View in Hangchow

Viewed from Coastal Tower, dawning hues look grand,
Along the dyke I tread on fine white sand.
At night General's Temple hears tides leap,
Spring dwells in Petite's Bower the willows sweep.
Her red sleeves weave brocade where flowers crop;
Blue streamers show amid pear blossoms a shop.
Who opens a southwest road to the temple?
Around a green skirt it slants like a girdle.

* Hangchow: the capital of today's Chechiang Province. The poet was its prefect from A.D. 822, the second year of Blessed One, to A.D. 824, the fourth year of Blessed One.
* Petite: Petite Su or Hsiaohsiao Su (A.D. 479 – A.D. 502), from Hangchow, a famous singer in Ch'i (A.D. 479 – A.D. 502) in the Southern Dynasties period.

别 州 民

耆老遮归路，
壶浆满别筵。
甘棠无一树，
那得泪潸然？
税重多贫户，
农饥足旱田。
唯留一湖水，
与汝救凶年。

Farewell to People of Hangchow

The old folk comes to bar my way;
Wine pot full filled, farewell he'd say.
Not fruit yet on the cherry tree,
Why do you in tears go from me?
Taxes heavy, no enough yield,
Starvelings all o'er the dried field.
But a lake of blue there remains
For you to pass the year in pains.

* Hangchow: the capital of today's Chechiang Province. The poet was its prefect from A.D. 822, the second year of Blessed One, to A.D. 824, the fourth year of Blessed One.
* cherry: any of various trees (genus *Prunus*) of the rose family, related to the plum and the peach and bearing small, round or heart-shaped drupes enclosing a smooth pit; especially the sweet cherry, the sour cherry and the wild black cherry.

白 云 泉

天平山上白云泉，
云自无心水自闲。
何必奔冲山下去？
更添波浪向人间！

White Cloud Fountain

The White Cloud Fountain flows from the Scale Hill!
Clouds are free of care; water flows at will.
Why rush down the mountain as if so hurled
To trouble waters in this human world?

* White Cloud Fountain: a fountain half way up the Scale Hill.
* the Scale Hill: west of Soochow, Chiangsu Province.

秋 雨 夜 眠

凉冷三秋夜,
安闲一老翁。
卧迟灯灭后,
睡美雨声中。
灰宿温瓶火,
香添暖被笼。
晓晴寒未起,
霜叶满阶红。

Sleeping on a Rainy Autumn Night

Cold, so cold, the late autumn night;
Free, so free, the old man at ease.
He goes to bed, gone off the light;
He now dreams of a rainy breeze.
Ember is kept well in the pot;
An incense cage perfumes the bed.
It's brisk at dawn — he rises not;
The maple leaves dye the steps red.

* incense cage: a cage usually made of bamboo holding incense burned slowly to perfume a bedroom in ancient China.
* maple: any of a large genus (*Acer*) of deciduous trees of the north temperate zone, with opposite leaves that turn red in autumn and a fruit of two joined samaras, a symbol of cordial love and good luck because of its bright fiery color.

与梦得沽酒闲饮且约后期

少时犹不忧生计,
老去谁能惜酒钱?
共把十千沽一斗,
相看七十欠三年。
闲征雅令穷经史,
醉听清吟胜管弦。
更待菊黄家酝熟,
共君一醉一陶然。

Drinking at Leisure Together with Dream Gained and Making an Appointment to Meet Again

While young, about life worried I was not.
Now old, how could I grudge buying wine?
Let's spend ten thousand on wine, a wine pot;
I'll be sixty-seven in two years in twine.
We read and play the drinkers' game for fun;
Drunk, better than the strings, I'd chant with you.
Chrysanthemums yellow and wine well done,
I will invite you to drink my home-brew.

* Dream Gained: the poet Yühsi Liu's courtesy name.
* chrysanthemum: any of a genus of perennials of the composite family, some cultivated varieties of which have large heads of showy flowers of various colors, a symbol of elegance and integrity in Chinese culture, one of the four most important floral images in Chinese literature, which are wintersweet, orchid, bamboo, and chrysanthemum.

览卢子蒙侍御旧诗，多与微之唱和，感今伤昔，因赠子蒙，题于卷后

早闻元九咏君诗，
恨与卢君相识迟。
今日逢君开旧卷，
卷中多道赠微之。
相看掩泪情难说，
别有伤心事岂知？
闻道咸阳坟上树，
已抽三丈白杨枝。

On Reading Tsumeng Lu's Old Poems Written in the Same Rhyming Scheme with Chen Yüan's, Usually in Response to Weitsu, So Moved, I Write This, Dedicated to Tsumeng, Inscribed at the End of the Chapter

Yesterday I've read Yüan's poem on you;
I have not known you till today I rue.
We read out your verse together today,
So many poems on friends passed away.
What can I say, looking at you in tears?
Who know how my heartaches for the past years?
I hear poplar trees in the Allshine grave
Have put forth long, long weeping twigs to wave.

* Yüan: Chen Yüan (A.D. 799 – A.D. 831), a famous T'ang poet, Pai's closest friend, the two forming a dyad in the history of Chinese Literature.
* Allshine: Allshine Town, the ancient capital of the State of Ch'in and later the Ch'in Empire, that is, present-day Hsienyang, Sha'anhsi Province.

红 鹦 鹉

安南远进红鹦鹉，
色似桃花语似人。
文章辩慧皆如此，
笼槛何年出得身？

The Red Parrot

Annam far has sent me a parrot red;
Hued like a peach flower, it mimics what's said.
It's learned and clever like you and me,
When on earth can it from the cage get free?

* parrot: the bird that can simulate human laughter and speech, having a hooked bill, paired toes, and usually brilliant plumage; a metaphor for the poet himself in this poem.
* Annam: the old name of Vietnam including today's Kuanghsi.

昼　卧

抱枕无言语，
空房独悄然。
谁知尽日卧，
非病亦非眠。

Lying in Bed at Daytime

My pillow in arms, nothing said,
My vacant room's silent for all.
From dawn to night I lie in bed;
Not ill, asleep I could not fall.

病中五绝(其五)

交亲不要苦相忧,
亦拟时时强出游。
但有心情何用脚?
陆乘肩舆水乘舟。

In Illness (No. 5)

My best friends need not worry about me;
I will take a walk, if from illness free.
I need not go on foot when going far;
Sedan car and boat, my good means they are.

杨 柳 枝 词

一树春风千万枝，
嫩如金色软于丝。
永丰西角荒园里，
尽日无人属阿谁？

Song of Willow Twigs

A tree of countless twigs in spring breeze sway,
Brighter than gold, softer than silks to play.
West of E'errich, in the park to decay,
Who'd come to view its beauty for the day?

* silk: the fine, soft, shiny fiber produced by silk worms to form their cocoons, and the thread or fabric made from this fibre is used as material for clothing. And it can be any clothing made of silk.
* E'errich: the name of a lane in Loshine.

忆 江 南

江南好，
风景旧曾谙。
日出江花红胜火，
春来江水绿如蓝。
能不忆江南？

Dreaming of South

The South's dear to me;
The scenes stay in my memory.
O'er the waves the sun glows, redder than fire;
The spring water flows, as blue as sapphire.
How can I not the South desire?

* South: generally the area south of the Yangtze River.
* sapphire: a translucent, transparent, deep-blue variety of corundum, valued as a precious stone.

长 相 思

汴水流，
泗水流，
流到瓜洲古渡头。
吴山点点愁。

思悠悠，
恨悠悠，
恨到归时方始休。
月明人倚楼。

Long Longing

The Pien waters flow,
The Ssu waters flow,
Flow to the old ferry of Kuachow.
The Woo-land hills bow in sorrow.

My rues grow and grow,
My woes grow and grow,
Grow until comes back my yokefellow.
We lean on the rail in moonglow.

* the Pien: a river originating from the northwest of Kaifeng, flowing into the Ssu River west of Hsuchow under today's Chiangsu Province.
* the Ssu: a river originating from Hsint'ai and flowing to Weishan Lake, 169 kilometers long, an important river in Shantung.
* Kuachow: literally, Melon Shoal, a town located in today's Yangchow, Chiangsu Province.

长　恨　歌

汉皇重色思倾国，
御宇多年求不得。
杨家有女初长成，
养在深闺人未识。
天生丽质难自弃，
一朝选在君王侧。
回眸一笑百媚生，
六宫粉黛无颜色。
春寒赐浴华清池，
温泉水滑洗凝脂。
侍儿扶起娇无力，
始是新承恩泽时。
云鬓花颜金步摇，
芙蓉帐暖度春宵。
春宵苦短日高起，
从此君王不早朝。
承欢侍宴无闲暇，
春从春游夜专夜。
后宫佳丽三千人，
三千宠爱在一身。
金屋妆成娇侍夜，
玉楼宴罢醉和春。
姊妹弟兄皆列土，
可怜光彩生门户。
遂令天下父母心，
不重生男重生女。
骊宫高处入青云，

仙乐风飘处处闻。
缓歌慢舞凝丝竹，
尽日君王看不足。
渔阳鼙鼓动地来，
惊破霓裳羽衣曲。
九重城阙烟尘生，
千乘万骑西南行。
翠华摇摇行复止，
西出都门百余里。
六军不发无奈何，
宛转蛾眉马前死。
花钿委地无人收，
翠翘金雀玉搔头。
君王掩面救不得，
回看血泪相和流。
黄埃散漫风萧索，
云栈萦纡登剑阁。
峨嵋山下少人行，
旌旗无光日色薄。
蜀江水碧蜀山青，
圣主朝朝暮暮情。
行宫见月伤心色，
夜雨闻铃肠断声。
天旋地转回龙驭，
到此踌躇不能去。
马嵬坡下泥土中，
不见玉颜空死处。
君臣相顾尽沾衣，
东望都门信马归。
归来池苑皆依旧，
太液芙蓉未央柳。

芙蓉如面柳如眉，
对此如何不泪垂。
春风桃李花开日，
秋雨梧桐叶落时。
西宫南内多秋草，
落叶满阶红不扫。
梨园弟子白发新，
椒房阿监青娥老。
夕殿萤飞思悄然，
孤灯挑尽未成眠。
迟迟钟鼓初长夜，
耿耿星河欲曙天。
鸳鸯瓦冷霜华重，
翡翠衾寒谁与共。
悠悠生死别经年，
魂魄不曾来入梦。
临邛道士鸿都客，
能以精诚致魂魄。
为感君王辗转思，
遂教方士殷勤觅。
排空驭气奔如电，
升天入地求之遍。
上穷碧落下黄泉，
两处茫茫皆不见。
忽闻海上有仙山，
山在虚无缥渺间。
楼阁玲珑五云起，
其中绰约多仙子。
中有一人字太真，
雪肤花貌参差是。
金阙西厢叩玉扃，

转教小玉报双成。
闻道汉家天子使,
九华帐里梦魂惊。
揽衣推枕起徘徊,
珠箔银屏迤逦开。
云鬓半偏新睡觉,
花冠不整下堂来。
风吹仙袂飘飖举,
犹似霓裳羽衣舞。
玉容寂寞泪阑干,
梨花一枝春带雨。
含情凝睇谢君王,
一别音容两渺茫。
昭阳殿里恩爱绝,
蓬莱宫中日月长。
回头下望人寰处,
不见长安见尘雾。
惟将旧物表深情,
钿合金钗寄将去。
钗留一股合一扇,
钗擘黄金合分钿。
但教心似金钿坚,
天上人间会相见。
临别殷勤重寄词,
词中有誓两心知。
七月七日长生殿,
夜半无人私语时。
在天愿作比翼鸟,
在地愿为连理枝。
天长地久有时尽,
此恨绵绵无绝期。

Lasting Grief

His Majesty's sought many years in vain
A beauty of beauties in his domain.
The Yang's have a girl just maturely grown,
Reared in her boudoir, to the world unknown.
Her inborn beauty is not to lie waste;
One day she's gained to the emperor's taste.
Her backward glance gives off a smiling grace,
Which fades all ladies of the royal race.
She's given a bath in Clean Pool, spring cold;
The spring smooths her skin, fairness manifold.
When she's helped out, tender and delicate,
The Crown alights for her, His fairest mate.
Her sable hair, rosy cheeks, supple gait;
Spring sees them in the scented bed till late.
The sun high, He hates a spring night's too short;
Henceforth He never minds the morning court.
So she attends feasts with Him in high glee;
They go on hikes and spend nights on the spree.
In the harem, of three thousand belles rare,
Only she indulges in His love and care.
Indoors, she dolls herself up for the night;
At feasts she makes Him drunk, a-beaming bright.
Her siblings all granted fiefs and ranks galore,
Resplendence tints her household, door to door.
Her parents render all parents on earth
To see their daughters as properties of worth.
The palace at Mt. Black Steed scrapes the sky;

Music there rings everywhere, low or high.
She dances to the slow tune the band plays;
All day long the enchanted crown there stays.
Then from Fishshine war drums thump, thump along;
And cut short *Plumage and Rainbow Dress Song*.
Dust veils the citadels from the ground;
Myriads of steeds and carts flee, southwest bound.
The royals run out with halts, up and down
Till they stop dozens of miles west of the town.
The six battalions lift up a war cry;
The culprit, His most favored, has to die.
Her ornaments so scattered, all there rolled,
Lo, her jade hairpin with a sparrow gold.
The Crown hides His face at her falling thud,
A-feeling His tears running with her blood.
The yellow dust whirls and the cold wind soughs;
Their path to Sword Gate Pass winds with clouds.
Near Mt. Brow souls are few and far between;
In the murk of dusk, the flags lose their sheen.
Shu's rivers are deep and her mountains blue,
But how can they compare with the Crown's rue?
The moon o'er Castle Pro Tem rends His heart;
The night rain hears the night toll, a blow smart.
The revolt crushed, to go back He'd speed gain;
He stops on Mawei Slope where she's been slain.
There's no trace in dust of how she appears;
He and the peer can't but burst into tears.
They look east to the capital again;
Urging their steeds, they give them a free rein.
The parks and pools are where they used to play;
By Nectar Pool the willows as e'er sway.

The spray like her brow, the lily her grace;
How can He hold back tears washing His face?
Spring zephyrs blow plums and peaches to bloom;
Autumn rains urge plane trees to meet their doom.
West Palace is now rank with autumn grass;
The fallen leaves dry no one sweeps, alas.
The boys, His drama mates, now grow gray hair,
The maids, once lithe at court, no longer fair.
The fireflies indoors set Him in thought deep;
His lamp dying out, He can't fall asleep.
Bells and drums slowly sound the night away;
The Milky Way shines to the break of day.
The frosted tiles are loving birds to pair;
The cold satin quilt, with whom could He share?
It's a long time since they parted, it seems,
But her spirit has ne'er haunted His dreams.
The capital has a Wordist in good faith,
Who's the power to control any wraith.
So moved by His Majesty's burning love,
The monk seeks for her below and above.
He plows through the air with lightning speed;
And searches the underworld with all heed.
He searches in Hades and the Realm of Bliss;
She's nowhere, his efforts going amiss.
Lo, he spots a fairy hill in the sea,
Which looks ethereal, not seeming to be.
Amid hued clouds exquisite castles loom,
Wherein dwell fairies like flowers in bloom.
Among them there is one, Great Truth by name;
As Belle Yang's her skin and face are the same.
At his knock opens West Camber golden;

To tell his presence he bids a maiden.
The news this maid brings from the emperor
Startles her dream neath her flowery cover.
Pushing her pillow, putting on her robe,
She gets up, swinging the ring on her lobe.
Her hair undone, half way she's from her sleep;
Her crown awry, her eyes to the hall peep.
She flutters her silk sleeves a breeze unfurls,
Like dancing in plumage, clinking with pearls.
Tears on her cheeks reveal her lonely gloom,
Like raindrops upon a pear sprig in bloom.
Ogling thru her sadness she thanks the Crown:
Since we parted, I've met none but my frown.
As our clinging love has been torn apart,
The days at Mt. Immortal gnaws my heart.
Looking to the world, the worldling's base,
I couldn't see Long Peace but dust and haze.
Since I could but voice my heart thru things old,
I'd send you an inlay and hairpin gold.
Before doing that, I broke both in twain,
On half to myself, the other to my swain.
May our hearts like inlays and gold be strong,
In Heaven or earth, we'll meet before long.
I told the angel while he turned to go:
The hearts beating at one rate should faith know.
On the seventh night of the seventh moon,
We'd in Immortal Hall murmur our boon.
Above, we'd be two birds of the same mind;
On earth, we'd be two branches intertwined.
Sky and earth will meet their end although vast;
Our sorrow lasts and will for ever last.

- Clean Pool: also known as Flora Pool in Flora Palace in one of the four most famous royal parks in China, built in the T'ang dynasty.
- Mt. Black Steed: the mountain south of Lintung, an important offset of Mt. Ch'in Ridge, 1,302 meters above sea level, the location of the royal palace of Ch'in and tomb of Emperor First.
- Fishshine: Fishshine Prefecture, which is today's Chi District, Tientsin, where Lushan An raised his banner of rebellion.
- *Plumage and Rainbow Dress Song*: *Plumage Dance* to be brief, a kind of court dance in the T'ang dynasty, to the accompaniment of a tune called *Rainbow Plumage*, which was believed to have been composed by Emperor Deepsire of T'ang.
- Sword Gate Pass: Sword Gate for short, a strategic pass with a plank road built along cliffs by Bright Chuke in the Three Kingdoms period, in present-day Ssuch'uan Province.
- Mt. Brow: one of the four Buddhist mountains, located in Ssuch'uan Province, named for its elegant brow-shaped silhouette viewed from a distance.
- Mawei Slope: the name of place west of Rising Peace, more than 30 miles from Long Peace.
- Nectar Pool: a pool, actually an artificial lake in Great Bright Palace.
- West Palace: West Interior Supreme Pole Palace, where Emperor Deepsire lived after his return from Shu.
- the Milky Way: the Silver River in Chinese mythology, a luminous band circling the heavens composed of stars and nebulae; the Galaxy. As legend goes, the Milky Way maid, the granddaughter of Emperor of Heaven fell in love with a worldly cowherd and they gave birth to a son and a daughter. When their love was disclosed to Emperor of Heaven, he sent Queen Mother to take the fairy back to Heaven. While Cowherd was trying to catch up in a boat the cow had made with its horn broken, Queen Mother rived the air with her hairpin, so there appeared the Silver River, i.e., the Milky Way to keep them apart, and the fairy and the cowherd became two stars called Vega and Altair.
- Wordist: one who believes in or professes belief of Wordism, the doctrines declared by Laocius (571 B.C.– 471 B.C.). In the T'ang dynasty, while Confucianism remained the guiding principle of state and social morality, Wordism had gathered an incrustation of mythology and superstition and became popular with both the court and the commoners. Laocius, the founder, was claimed by the reigning dynasty as its remote progenitor and was honored with an imperial title, Emperor Dark One.
- Hades: the abode of the dead, and a euphemism for hell.
- the Realm of Bliss: a Chinese term for Heaven or the sky.

* West Chamber: a west hall of a castle in Heaven.
* Mt. Immortal: the Fairy Isles in East Sea.
* Long Peace: Ch'ang'an if transliterated, the metropolis of gold, the capital of the T'ang Empire, with 1,000,000 inhabitants, the largest walled city ever built by man, and now the capital of today's Sha'anhsi Province. Long Peace saw the wonder of Chinese civilization that reached the pinnacle of brilliance in Emperor Deepsire's reign.
* the Lord: Heng Li (A.D. 711 – A.D. 762), Emperor Deepsire's third son, the 7th emperor of T'ang, who was enthroned during Lushan An's Rebellion.
* Immortal Hall: In Flora Palace on Mt. Black Steed, built in A.D. 742.

池　　上

小娃撑小艇，
偷采白莲回。
不解藏踪迹，
浮萍一道开。

On the Pool

The small child rows a smaller yacht;
Lotus buds stolen, he does slide.
How to hide his trace he knows not;
Where he is, duckweed floats aside.

* lotus: any of various waterlilies, especially the white or pink Asian lotus, used as a religious symbol in Hinduism and Buddhism. The lotus is a common image in Chinese literature, as two lines of a lyric by Hsiu Ouyang (A.D. 1007 - A.D. 1072) read: "A thunder brings rain to the wood and pool, / The rain hushes the lotus, drips cool.
* duckweed: any of several small, disk-shaped, floating aquatic plants common in streams and ponds.

喜　雨

圃旱忧葵堇，
农旱忧禾菽。
人各有所私，
我旱忧松竹。
松干竹焦死，
眷眷在心目。
洒叶溉其根，
汲水劳僮仆。
油云忽东起，
凉雨凄相续。
似面洗垢尘，
如头得膏沐。
千柯习习润，
万叶欣欣绿。
十日浇灌功，
不如一霢霂。
方知宰生灵，
何异活草木。
所以圣与贤，
同心调玉烛。

A Blessing Rain

Lands and gardens yearn for a rain;
All farmers care about their grain.
Every man has his own concern;

Pine and bamboo all seem to burn.
Seeing the drought dry them away
I can't help worrying night and day.
"Cover the roots with leaves that fall",
"Get some water", to lads I call.
Heavy clouds pop up from the east,
Bringing with them a drizzling feast.
It's like a bath washing off dust,
Or air sending a soothing gust.
Hundreds of twigs sweet rains nourish;
Thousands of leaves start to flourish.
Ten days' watering hour by hour
Cannot compare with a sweet shower.
Now I know what governs the masses
Is no different from growing grasses.
So all saints, sages and all men right,
Please trim and set your candle bright.

* pine: any of a genus (*Pinus*) of evergreen trees of the pine family, a cone-bearing tree having bundles of two to five needle-shaped leaves growing in clusters, an important image in Chinese literature, a symbol of rectitude, longevity and so on.
* bamboo: a tall, tree-like or shrubby grass in tropical and semi-tropical regions, a symbol of integrity, fortitude and altitude. A Ching poet speaks of its character in a poem *Bamboo Rooted in the Rock*: "You bite the green hill and ne'er rest. / Roots in the broken crag, you grow, / And stand erect although hard pressed. /East, west, south, north, let the wind blow."

村 居 苦 寒

八年十二月，
五日雪纷纷。
竹柏皆冻死，
况彼无衣民。
回观村闾间，
十室八九贫。
北风利如剑，
布絮不蔽身。
唯烧蒿棘火，
愁坐夜待晨。
乃知大寒岁，
农者尤苦辛。
顾我当此日，
草堂深掩门。
褐裘覆絁被，
坐卧有馀温。
幸免饥冻苦，
又无垄亩勤。
念彼深可愧，
自问是何人？

Bitter Winter in the Village

The twelfth moon of the eighth year,
It snowed heavily for days five;
E'en bamboos and pines died, drear;

Unclad, how can folks stay alive?
To have a look I went around;
One eighth or so had not enough.
North wind cut with a rasping sound,
Their bodies in no clothes e'en rough.
They burned thistle and grass, behold,
Crouched waiting for the sun to rise.
In such a bitter winter cold,
The peasant suffered many tries;
I look at myself just today;
Closed is my thatched hall, tight the door.
My fur's on the silk overlay;
Where'er I am, I'm warm and more.
No hunger or cold can fret me;
No need for me to work the land.
Ashamed, I ask: who could I be,
In this dust world able to stand?

* bamboos and pines: a metonymy for plants.
* thistle: any of various plants of the composite family, with prickly leaves and heads of white, purple, pink, or yellow flowers.
* silk: the fine, soft, shiny fiber produced by silk worms to form their cocoons, and the thread or fabric made from this fibre is used as material for clothing. And it can be any clothing made of silk.

宿紫阁山北村

晨游紫阁峰，
暮宿山下村。
村老见余喜，
为余开一尊。
举杯未及饮，
暴卒来入门。
紫衣挟刀斧，
草草十馀人。
夺我席上酒，
掣我盘中飧。
主人退后立，
敛手反如宾。
中庭有奇树，
种来三十春。
主人惜不得，
持斧断其根。
口称采造家，
身属神策军。
主人慎勿语，
中尉正承恩。

A Night at North Village in Mt. Purple Tower

Morn and I stroll Mt. Purple Tower;
Dusk and I for the night put up.

In the village, where the old man
Is pleased to offer me a cup.
Before we drink though cups are raised,
There in burst some fierce and rough men.
In purple, carrying axes and swords.
Such grabbing wolves count more than ten.
They seize our wine and devour all;
What is in the plate they molest.
My host steps back, stands there and bows
As if he were their polite guest.
In his mid-yard stands a fine tree
For thirty years cared for by him;
He does love it with all his heart;
The roughs fell it and the roots trim.
"We are sent by the court for wood;
We are the Emperor's guards ace."
So I tell the host not to talk
For their captain enjoys His grace.

* Mt. Purple Tower: the head of the South Hills, 15 kilometers from Long Peace.
* wolf: a large carnivorous mammal related to the dog, regarded as ravenous, cruel, or rapacious, a metaphor for an invader or lecher in Chinese culture.

观 刈 麦

田家少闲月，
五月人倍忙。
夜来南风起，
小麦覆陇黄。
妇姑荷箪食，
童稚携壶浆，
相随饷田去，
丁壮在南冈。
足蒸暑土气，
背灼炎天光，
力尽不知热，
但惜夏日长。
复有贫妇人，
抱子在其旁，
右手秉遗穗，
左臂悬敝筐。
听其相顾言，
闻者为悲伤。
家田输税尽，
拾此充饥肠。
今我何功德，
曾不事农桑。
吏禄三百石，
岁晏有馀粮。
念此私自愧，
尽日不能忘。

Watching the Wheat Reapers

Farmers have but little free time,
And the fifth moon busiest they are.
At night wind blows from the south clime
And wheat turns to gold near and far.
Wives and girls with carrying food,
Children with water pots in hand,
Stream out to the fields as they would
To serve the lads working the land.
Heat from soil burns the reapers' feet;
On their back like fire plays the sun.
So busy, they don't care the heat
But fear that the sun sets anon.
And then a poor woman I see
Carrying her child on her back.
In her right hand gleaned ears there be,
In her left a worn basket black.
I feel sad as she speaks to me:
"All goes for taxes; no crops will
Be left there to my family.
But gleanings can my stomach fill!"
What virtue or worth have I here?
I ne'er till or rake the fields, ne'er.
I've three hundred piculs each year,
Enough to eat with much to spare;
At this I feel shame right away;
And this I can't forget all day.

* wheat: a grain yielding an edible flour, the annual product of a cereal grass (genus *Triticum*), introduced to China from West Asia more than 4,000 years ago, used as a staple food in China and most of the world. In its importance to consumers, it is second only to rice.
* picul: a unit of weight, a hundred catties or 50 kilograms.

大　水

浔阳郊郭间，
大水岁一至。
闾阎半飘荡，
城堞多倾坠。
苍茫生海色，
渺漫连空翠。
风卷白波翻，
日煎红浪沸。
工商彻屋去，
牛马登山避。
况当率税时，
颇害农桑事。
独有佣舟子，
鼓枻生意气。
不知万人灾，
自觅锥刀利。
吾无奈尔何，
尔非久得志。
九月霜降后，
水涸为平地。

The Flood

Each year in Bankshine, field or lane
There comes a deluge all to drown.
The homes in water there remain,

And collapse the walls of the town.
All's changed with the flood like a sea;
Outside so green everything seems;
As winds rise, white waves leap so free;
The flood turns red as the sun beams;
Craftsmen and traders leave their town;
Cattle and sheep are moved uphill;
This is the time taxes are drawn,
Bad to farming, and farmers still.
But boatmen are happy to gain;
More opportunities they take.
They worry not o'er those in pain,
Just keen on the profits they make;
Can they always have a good sum?
Their happiness will soon degrade;
After the ninth moon frosts will come;
Waters drying will end their trade.

* Bankshine: a former name of the Nine Rivers, which is today's Ch'iuchiang, Chianghsi Province.
* cattle: farm animals collectively, usually referring to oxen collective, livestock.
* sheep: a medium-sized domesticated ruminant of the genus *Ovis*, highly prized for its flesh, wool and skin, regarded as meek and mild, a symbol of beauty and purity, used as a sacrifice in both Western and Eastern cultures.

新 制 布 裘

桂布白似雪，
吴绵软于云。
布重绵且厚，
为裘有馀温。
朝拥坐至暮，
夜覆眠达晨。
谁知严冬月，
支体暖如春。
中夕忽有念，
抚裘起逡巡。
丈夫贵兼济，
岂独善一身。
安得万里裘，
盖裹周四垠。
稳暖皆如我，
天下无寒人。

My New Gown

Snow white cloth used for a new gown,
Soft as clouds padding's sewn inside.
The cotton makes padding like down;
Warm all day, in warmth I abide.
All day long I wear the gown mere,
And with it I sleep till birds sing.
Who'd think in the end of the year

I'd be warm as if it were spring?
Once I awake on a deep night;
The gown speaks suddenly to me:
A hero should be high and right;
Can he stand alone, how can he?
Where can I get cloth wide and free
To cover the whole of the Land?
So that all will be warm like me
And no one will in cold air stand?

* cotton: the soft, white seed hairs filling the seedpods of various shrubby plants of the mallow family, originally native to the tropics, introduced to China in the Western Han dynasty.

纳　　粟

有吏夜叩门，
高声催纳粟。
家人不待晓，
场上张灯烛。
扬簸净如珠，
一车三十斛。
犹忧纳不中，
鞭责及僮仆。
昔余谬从事，
内愧才不足。
连授四命官，
坐尸十年禄。
常闻古人语，
损益周必复。
今日谅甘心，
还他太仓谷。

Collecting Grain Tax

At night, a loud bang on the door,
"Grain tax", a collector does roar.
Before the morning comes around；
I light up the threshing ground.
Grain's winnowed until pearls there are,
Thirty qeufs are good for a car.
Worrying it's not an enough load,

My boy servant now I do goad.
I was an official before;
I feel ashamed with such a sore.
I was promoted for four tiers,
And enjoyed good pay for ten years;
Old folks, as said once and again,
Can tell the moon's rise, wax and wane.
Now I wish I could give back all
To the barn in the capital.

* pearl: a smooth, lustrous, usually white and bluish-gray, calcareous concretion deposited in layers around a central nucleus in the shells of various mollusks or oysters, and largely used as a gem, medicine or given as a gift, representing nobility, purity and dignity in Chinese culture.
* qeuf: a measure used in ancient times for measurement of grain, about 60 kilograms.

采 地 黄 者

麦死春不雨，
禾损秋早霜。
岁晏无口食，
田中采地黄。
采之将何用，
持以易馋粮。
凌晨荷锄去，
薄暮不盈筐。
携来朱门家，
卖与白面郎。
与君啖肥马，
可使照地光。
愿易马残粟，
救此苦饥肠。

The Rehmannia Gatherer

Wheat parched, still there is no spring rain;
White frosts fall to the Crops in pain.
Year o'er, we have got no good yield;
Some dig rehmannia in the field.
What is that used for? Is that good?
It is to be bartered for food.
Out they go, shouldering a hoe;
Back they come, no full baskets show.
To sell, to the great house they walk;

To win, with the fair face they talk.
Eating this, your horse will grow fat,
With luster lighting all like that.
You can pay me in waste horse grain
So that we can ourselves sustain.

* rehmannia: *rehmannia glutinosa*, a perennial plant of the figwort root family, used as herbal medicine.

赠友诗五首(选二)
To My Friend (Two out of Five)

其　三

私家无钱炉,
平地无铜山。
胡为秋夏税,
岁岁输铜钱。
钱力日已重,
农力日已殚。
贱粜粟与麦,
贱贸丝与绵。
岁暮衣食尽,
焉得无饥寒。
吾闻国之初,
有制垂不刊。
庸必算丁口,
租必计桑田。
不求土所无,
不强人所难。
量入以为出,
上足下亦安。
兵兴一变法,
兵息遂不还。
使我农桑人,
憔悴畎亩间。
谁能革此弊,
待君秉利权。

复彼租庸法，
令如贞观年。

No. 3

None private can mint coin or bills;
No plains show copper-mining hills;
Why all taxation, there and here?
Demands are made from year to year.
No money do we have to spend,
And now the year comes to an end.
Millet and wheat are sold, so cheap
Cotton and silk for sale, they weep.
The year's gone, and products all sold;
How can we bear hunger and cold?
I hear when the state had its base,
Rules were made and offered was grace.
Each folk was counted as a hand;
All lots rented were seen as land.
What the land had not was not sought;
What a hand could not was just aught.
All people could make both ends meet;
The state stayed staid, the folks felt sweet.
In war time, the system was changed;
When peace came, all kept disarranged.
We farmers suffered every pain
In each field and upon each lane.
To undo this who could arrange?
May the lord use his power to change.
May law be restored, all well done,
Back to the years of Right Begun.

* Written in his Brushwood days in the year of 808.
* millet: a member of the foxtail grass family, or its seeds, culvivated as a cereal, used as a stable food in ancient times, having been cultivated in China for more than 7,300 years, one of the earliest crops in the world.
* wheat: a grain yielding an edible flour, the annual product of a cereal grass (genus *Triticum*), introduced to China from West Asia more than 4,000 years ago, used as a staple food in China and most of the world. In its importance to consumers, it is second only to rice.
* cotton: the soft, white seed hairs filling the seedpods of various shrubby plants of the mallow family, originally native to the tropics, introduced to China in the Western Han dynasty. The seeds can be made into oil and the fiber velvet into cloth.
* silk: the fine, soft, shiny fiber produced by silk worms to form their cocoons, and the thread or fabric made from this fibre is used as material for clothing.
* Right Begun: Right Begun (A. D. 627 - A.D. 650) refers to the reign title of Emperor Firstsire of the T'ang Dynasty. During this period, effective policies and good government led to population growth and the rapid development of the feudal economy. Thus early historians referred to the Right Begun reign as "a period of enlightened administration".

其 五

三十男有室，
二十女有归。
近代多离乱，
婚姻多过期。
嫁娶既不早，
生育常苦迟。
儿女未成人，
父母已衰羸。
凡人贵达日，
多在长大时。
欲报亲不待，
孝心无所施。
哀哉三牲养，
少得及庭闱。
惜哉万钟粟，
多用饱妻儿。
谁能正婚礼，
待君张国维。
庶使孝子心，
皆无风树悲。

No. 5

Men married at thirty years old;
Girls left at twenty, a new mold.
Today people all flee their clime;
No all marriage can come in time.
With no proper conjugal life,

It is hard for husband and wife.
Before their children come of age
The parent are in their last stage.
One can have most riches and power
When his life does begin to flower.
My parents I'd like to repay,
But no way as they've passed away.
So sad, those who have a good pay
Don't give their parents a good ray.
So bad, those who lead a good life
Spend too much on their kids and wife.
Who can set our customs all right;
Can you make our land a good sight?
Do serve you parents well enow
In case the trees should sadly sough.

开龙门八节石滩二首
Dredging Eight Stone Rapids at Dragongate, Two Poems

其 一

铁凿金锤殷若雷,
八滩九石剑棱摧。
竹篙桂楫飞如箭,
百筏千艘鱼贯来。
振锡导师凭众力,
挥金退傅施家财。
他时相逐西方去,
莫虑尘沙路不开。

No. 1

Chisels and hammers thump, playing their part;
Eight rapids and nine rocks are crushed to none.
Bamboo poles and laurel oars forward dart.
All rafts and yachts ahead rush one by one.
Each monk and priest to help will do their best;
All I have, property and gold, I'll spend.
When one day I leave the world for the west,
I won't worry, the road will far extend.

---

* Dragongate: one of the Four Grottoes in China, located in Loshine under today's Honan Province.
* chisels and hammers: referring to the tools used in the hydraulic project.

其 二

七十三翁旦暮身，
誓开险路作通津。
夜舟过此无倾覆，
朝胫从今免苦辛。
十里叱滩变河汉，
八寒阴狱化阳春。
我身虽殁心长在，
暗施慈悲与后人。

No. 2

I, in my last days at seventy-three,
Swear to set the track right and the gorge free.
So that no boats will overturn at night
And no one will e'er trudge in dawning light.
The long rapids will be the Milky Way;
The cold Hades will enjoy its spring day.
E'en if I die, my heart will long remain;
Our descendants can have good shine and rain.

* Written in A.D. 844 in Loshine two years before the poet's death, these two poems explaining how the Dragongate hydraulic project was carried out. The river referred to is the Yia tributary of the Lo after which Loshine was named. In the absence of good highways boats were used to transport heavy cargo such as grain over long distances. These waterways were particularly important in time of war.
* Dragongate: one of the Four Grottoes in China, located in Loshine under today's Honan Province.
* the Milky Way: the Silver River in Chinese mythology, a luminous band circling the heavens composed of stars and nebulae; the Galaxy. As legend goes, the Milky Way

maid, the granddaughter of Emperor of Heaven fell in love with a worldly cowherd and they gave birth to a son and a daughter. When their love was disclosed to Emperor of Heaven, he sent Queen Mother to take the fairy back to Heaven. While Cowherd was trying to catch up in a boat the cow had made with its horn broken, Queen Mother rived the air with her hair pin, so there appeared the Silver River, i.e., the Milky Way to keep them apart, and the fairy and the cowherd became two stars called Vega and Altair.

* Hades: the abode of the dead, and a euphemism for hell.

折 剑 头

拾得折剑头,
不知折之由。
一握青蛇尾,
数寸碧峰头。
疑是斩鲸鲵,
不然刺蛟虬。
缺落泥土中,
委弃无人收。
我有鄙介性,
好刚不好柔。
勿轻直折剑,
犹胜曲全钩。

A Broken Sword

A broken sword there was I found;
I did not know why it lay aground.
In my hand it looked like a snake;
Its edge's serrated like a rake.
Is it because it stabbed a whale
Or once cut off a dragon's tail?
It was thrown to the soil alone;
Such a thing no one would fain own.
I have a peculiar hard trait;
A hard nut outdoes a soft date.
Do not despise it for its look;

<blockquote>
It's better than a perfect hook.
</blockquote>

* snake: an ophidian reptile, having a greatly elongated, scaly body, no limbs, and a specialized swallowing apparatus, a symbol of indifference, malevolence, cattiness, and craftiness in Chinese culture.
* whale: a cetaceous mammal of fish-like form, as distinguished from dolphins and porpoises. It is a symbol of great ambition, fortitude and uniqueness, and sometimes of an impending threat.
* date: an oblong, sweet, fleshy fruit of the date palm, enclosing a single hard seed, a symbol of early fertility in Chinese culture.

放　　鹰

十月鹰出笼，
草枯雉兔肥。
下鞲随指顾，
百掷无一遗。
鹰翅疾如风，
鹰爪利如锥。
本为鸟所设，
今为人所资。
孰能使之然，
有术甚易知。
取其向背性，
制在饥饱时。
不可使长饱，
不可使长饥。
饥则力不足，
饱则背人飞。
乘饥纵搏击，
未饱须縶维。
所以爪翅功，
而人坐收之。
圣明驭英雄，
其术亦如斯。
鄙语不可弃，
吾闻诸猎师。

Letting Out the Falcon

The tenth moon, the falcon's let out,
Pheasants and hares fat, grass about.
Where the hunter points, it does dart,
Leaving nothing uncaught, so smart.
Its wings as swift as a north blast;
Its claws as sharp as a hook cast;
Wings and claws are for birds, that kind,
Now used by men, as is designed.
How can a falcon be well trained?
That is easy if the knack's gained:
Look at its likes, dislikes, that lot,
And when it's hungry, when it's not.
Ne'er let it eat to its desire,
Nor let it starve lest it expire.
Ill fed, it has not strength to prey;
Well fed, from you it'll fly away.
When it's hungry, let it attack;
Ere it eats enough, have it back.
The power of its claws and its wings
Are your property, are your things.
How does a sovereign command?
The art is just like this, if scanned.
What I've said you should not despise;
It's something heard from hunters wise.

---

* falcon: any bird of prey with long pointed wings and a short, curved, notched beak, usually trained to hunt and kill small game. In falconry, the female is called a falcon

and the male a tiercel.
* pheasant: a long-tailed gallinaceous bird noted for the gorgeous plumage of the male, often regarded as wild chiken in Chinese culture.
* hare: a rodent (genus *Lepus*) with cleft upper lip, long ears, and long hind legs — characterized by its timidity and swiftness, habitating woodland, farmland or grassland.

紫　　藤

藤花紫蒙茸，
藤叶青扶疏。
谁谓好颜色，
而为害有馀。
下如蛇屈盘，
上若绳紫纡。
可怜中间树，
束缚成枯株。
柔蔓不自胜，
袅袅挂空虚。
岂知缠树木，
千夫力不如。
先柔后为害，
有似谀佞徒。
附著君权势，
君迷不肯诛。
又如妖妇人，
绸缪蛊其夫。
奇邪坏人室，
夫惑不能除。
寄言邦与家，
所慎在其初。
毫末不早辨，
滋蔓信难图。
愿以藤为诫，
铭之于座隅。

Wisteria

Wisteria flowers, a velvet show,
Green leaves like wind sway to and fro.
Who'd think that the plant with such charm
Could bring about a serious harm?
When it grows, it coils like a snake
Upward growing for coiling's sake.
The tree it entwines low and high
Is strangled and choked as to die.
Too soft and delicate to stand,
It hangs in the void o'er the land.
Once it does cling fast to a tree,
A thousand men can't get it free;
At first soft, then it's a bad flower,
Like the crafty courtiers in power.
So favored by the throne they sway,
Obsessed, the throne will not them slay.
And it's like a bewitching wife
That charms him and destroys his life.
Her foolish man does not know this
And won't rid her though bad she is.
A word for a home and a state,
Take care, don't hesitate till late.
Small faults if you do not discern,
Worse and worst they will tend to turn.
Wisteria's Lesson One for me;
I'll keep this verse, as will long be.

* wisteria: any of a genus *Wisteria* of woody twining shrubs of the bean family, with pinnate leaves, elongated pods, and handsome clusters of blue, purple, or white flowers.
* snake: an ophidian reptile, having a greatly elongated, smooth and cold scaly body, no limbs, and a specialized swallowing apparatus, a symbol of indifference, malevolence, cattiness, and craftiness in Chinese culture.
* Lesson One: a metaphor, the very first lesson that one should learn.

悲 哉 行

悲哉为儒者,
力学不知疲。
读书眼欲暗,
秉笔手生胝。
十上方一第,
成名常苦迟。
纵有宦达者,
两鬓已成丝。
可怜少壮日,
适在穷贱时。
丈夫老且病,
焉用富贵为。
沉沉朱门宅,
中有乳臭儿。
状貌如妇人,
光明膏粱肌。
手不把书卷,
身不擐戎衣。
二十袭封爵,
门承勋戚资。
春来日日出,
服御何轻肥。
朝从博徒饮,
暮有倡楼期。
平封还酒债,
堆金选蛾眉。
声色狗马外,

其馀一无知。
山苗与涧松，
地势随高卑。
古来无奈何，
非君独伤悲。

O Sad

A scholar, ne'er tired of work, he
Read a book till he could not see.
Wielding his brush while he did stand
Until calloused became his hand.
For ten times he's taken Grand Test,
And passed it too late, so hard pressed.
Though he's in office on the height,
His two sideburns have now grown white.
What a pity, when in full prime,
He was poor, having a hard time.
Now old and oft sick he does rue:
What can riches and honors do?
In the house red-roofed and red-tiled,
There is a stripling, a wet child.
He looks like a girl with soft skin,
A shining face, a shining grin.
He has never picked up a book,
Or worn an armor for that look.
At twenty he inherits peer,
With merits, riches, honors sheer!
Spring coming, he comes out to course,
In furs, and riding a sleek horse.

He gambles and drinks and cash hurls,
And in pubs sleeping with the girls.
He spends his wealth paying wine bills,
And for belles piles money like hills.
Besides carousing and hunting,
Nothing he knows, he knows nothing.
The hill sees grass grow neath a pine;
The terrain does rise and decline.
From olden times it's been this way;
It's not yourself that sigh today.

* Grand Test: referring to imperial civil-service examinations for selecting talents to serve as meritocratic governmental officials, a system and practice initiated in the Han dynasty (202 B.C.– A.D. 220), formally begun in the Sui dynasty (A.D. 581 – A.D. 619), well-developed in the T'ang dynasty (A.D. 618 – A.D. 907) and abolished in the Late Ch'ing dynasty (A.D. 1636 – A.D. 1912). Those who passed the enteree (chin shih) level were indeed given upper-echelon government appointments, and as a perk, they were generally allied by marriage to upper-crust families. In the eighteenth century, the Jesuits and their friend Voltaire recommended such a system for Europe as a safety valve for Europe's ossified social structure, which was soon overthrown by waves of aristocratic blood.
* horse: a large solid-hoofed quadruped (*Equus caballus*) with coarse mane and tail, of various strains: Ferghana, Mongolian, Kazaks, Hequ, Karasahr and so on and of various colors: black, white, yellow, brown, dappled and so on, commonly in the domesticated state, employed as a beast of draught and burden and especially for riding upon.
* pine: a cone-bearing evergreen tree having needle-shaped leaves growing in clusters, a symbol of rectitude, fortitude and longevity in Chinese culture.

杏园中枣树

人言百果中,
唯枣凡且鄙。
皮皴似龟手,
叶小如鼠耳。
胡为不自知,
生花此园里。
岂宜遇攀玩,
幸免遭伤毁。
二月曲江头,
杂英红旖旎。
枣亦在其间,
如嫫对西子。
东风不择木,
吹煦长未已。
眼看欲合抱,
得尽生生理。
寄言游春客,
乞君一回视。
君爱绕指柔,
从君怜柳杞。
君求悦目艳,
不敢争桃李。
君若作大车,
轮轴材须此。

The Date Tree in the Apricot Orchard

As said, of a hundred fruits raised,
The date is common and abased.
Its bark as wrinkled as hands chapped;
Its leaves as small as rat's ears mapped.
Your own status, why don't you know?
Why come to this orchard to grow?
How can you bear all climb and play?
So lucky, free from harm you stay.
The second moon comes to the Bent;
No blossoming one can prevent.
Among them the date tree does fade,
Like a crone facing West Maid.
The east wind does not choose to blow,
Blowing to all trees that there grow.
The tree will be thick, armful soon,
Having all of natural boon.
To the tourists I would now say
Please look aback or you can stay.
If you treasure what's soft and thin,
You may love willows' smile to win.
To seek what's pleasing if you come,
It will not vie with peach and plum.
If you'd like to make a big car;
It is the best wood, here you are!

* date: an oblong, sweet, fleshy fruit of the date palm, enclosing a single hard seed, a symbol of early fertility in Chinese culture. A tree that bears such fruit.

* apricot: a tree or the fruit of the tree of the rose family, intermediate between the peach and the plum. Growing, reaping or selling apricots alludes to a hermit who is kind to the folks, just like Feng Tung, who gave free medical treatment to them except that he asked them to plant one to five apricot trees for him according to the severity of their illness.
* the Bent: Ch'uchiang if transliterated, a royal park of T'ang, located in the southeast of Long Peace, the capital.
* West Maid: a famed beauty of the Spring and Autumn Period. Once a laundry lady in the State of Yüeh, which was then a tributary to the State of Wu. Because of her beauty, West Maid was selected to be trained in Yüeh's palace, and sent to King of Wu as a spy. Immediately, she won the king's affection and favor with her bewitching charm and performance art of dancing. As a result, the State of Wu waned and perished.
* willow: any of a large genus of shrubs and trees related to the poplars, having generally smooth branches, and often long, slender, pliant, and sometimes pendent branchlets, a symbol of farewell or nostalgia in Chinese culture.
* peach: any of the plant (*Prunus Percica*), bearing a fleshy, juicy, edible drupe, cultivated in many varieties in temperate zones considered sacred in China, often used as a metaphor for a young woman, as a section of a poem in *The Book of Songs* reads: The peach twigs sway, / Ablaze the flower; / Now she's married away, / Befitting her new bower."
* plum: a kind of plant or the edible purple drupaceous fruit of the plant which is any one of various trees of the genus *Prunus*, cultivated in temperate zones.

梦　　仙

人有梦仙者，
梦身升上清。
坐乘一白鹤，
前引双红旌。
羽衣忽飘飘，
玉鸾俄铮铮。
半空直下视，
人世尘冥冥。
渐失乡国处，
才分山水形。
东海一片白，
列岳五点青。
须臾群仙来，
相引朝玉京。
安期羡门辈，
列侍如公卿。
仰谒玉皇帝，
稽首前致诚。
帝言汝仙才，
努力勿自轻。
却后十五年，
期汝不死庭。
再拜受斯言，
既寤喜且惊。
秘之不敢泄，
誓志居岩扃。
恩爱舍骨肉，

饮食断膻腥。
朝餐云母散，
夜吸沆瀣精。
空山三十载，
日望辎軿迎。
前期过已久，
鸾鹤无来声。
齿发日衰白，
耳目减聪明。
一朝同物化，
身与粪壤并。
神仙信有之，
俗力非可营。
苟无金骨相，
不列丹台名。
徒传辟谷法，
虚受烧丹经。
只自取勤苦，
百年终不成。
悲哉梦仙人，
一梦误一生。

Dreaming of Being an Immortal

One dreams he an immortal be,
Rising, rising to the great blue.
Astride a white crane he does ride,
Led along by red banners two.
Magic birds sing their dulcet song;
His robe billows out as he flies.

The world down below is all haze,
As he looks half way from the skies.
In mountains and rivers below,
He can't discern his home between.
East Sea is like a sheet of white;
The Five Mountains are but spots green;
Soon a great crowd of spirits come
And lead him to the Lord of Jade;
He admires those seated in line,
Like grandees there to serve and aid.
As they stand worshiping the throne,
He proceeds ahead to kowtow.
The Lord of Jade says: "You're a god.
Do not demean yourself here now!
You'll live on earth fifteen years more.
Before you come back to the skies."
At this the man bows down again,
Between delight and much surprise.
Keeping his secret to himself,
He leaves home and goes to the wood.
Deserting his dear wife and kids,
Having no meat or fish for food.
He chews powdered mica at dawn
And breathes in mist and dew at night;
For thirty years he lives this way,
Waiting for Lord of Jade to light.
After fifteen years he wonders:
Why hasn't even the crane come.
His teeth fallen, his hair grown gray,
He's nearly blind and almost numb.
At last, like all things dead, he dies;

His body turning into none.
If spirits and gods do exist,
A common one cannot be one.
If you're not made of stuff divine,
Your dream of Red Shrine won't come true.
Don't waste your life to seek in vain;
Elixir's not been made for you.
Even if you practise for long;
You will not succeed, not at all.
Pity, he who'd immortal be;
In an empty dream is to fall.

* crane: one of a family of large, long-necked, long-legged, heronlike birds allied to the rails, a symbol of integrity and longevity in Chinese culture, only second to the phoenix in cultural importance.
* East Sea: what is known as East China Sea today, with an area of 770 thousand square kilometers.
* the Five Mountains: the five famous mountains in China including Mount Ever in Shanhsi, Mount Scale in Hunan, Mount Arch in Shantung, Mount Flora in Sha'anhsi, and Mount Tower in Honan, which symbolizes the unity of the Chinese nation from north, south, east, west and the central part.
* Lord of Jade: the deity of highest power in Chinese mythology, identifiable with the Word or God in western culture for having the same attributes as omnipresence, omniscience and omnipotence and being personal as the ultimate sovereign of all, living and non-living.
* mica: a mineral called silicate in various shapes and hues, having natural veins or lines like a painting, which may be colorless, jet-black, transparent or translucent.
* Red Shrine: the abode for immortals.
* elixir: a hypothetical substance sought by medical alchemists to change base metals into gold or prolong life indefinitely.

凶　　宅

长安多大宅，
列在街西东。
往往朱门内，
房廊相对空。
枭鸣松桂枝，
狐藏兰菊丛。
苍苔黄叶地，
日暮多旋风。
前主为将相，
得罪窜巴庸。
后主为公卿，
寝疾殁其中。
连延四五主，
殃祸继相钟。
自从十年来，
不利主人翁。
风雨坏檐隙，
蛇鼠穿墙墉。
人疑不敢买，
日毁土木功。
嗟嗟俗人心，
甚矣其愚蒙。
但恐灾将至，
不思祸所从。
我今题此诗，
欲悟迷者胸。
凡为大官人，

年禄多高崇。
权重持难久,
位高势易穷。
骄者物之盈,
老者数之终。
四者如寇盗,
日夜来相攻。
假使居吉土,
孰能保其躬?
因小以明大,
借家可喻邦。
周秦宅崤函,
其宅非不同。
一兴八百年;
一死望夷宫。
寄语家与国,
人凶非宅凶。

The Haunted Estate

Long Peace boasts many mansions great,
A-lining both sides of each street.
Behold, behind their great red gates,
Each room empty for someone waits.
On the pine branch an owl perches;
Neath wild orchids a fox searches.
Moss and yellow leaves strew the ground;
The dusk wind whirls round after round.
The first host, premier, was exiled
To Pa and Yung, the areas wild.

The next was a prince who is dead,
Having lain for some time in bed.
Then four or five owners did come,
Who did to disasters succumb.
For about ten years on the run.
It has harmed owners one by one.
With no upkeep the eaves will fall;
Rats and snakes dig holes in the wall.
No one dare buy it, full of doubt;
Bricks, tiles and timber rot about.
All men are fools in this world vain,
Their souls the worldly dust does stain.
They fear troubles fall from the sky,
But ne'er ask themselves of the why.
I am writing this poem today
To enlighten those gone astray.
All those who sway their greatest power
Have great pay and riches to tower.
Those in power can't power long retain;
From above they'll drop, poor again.
A proud man, who cannot all spend
Will with his age comes to an end.
Thieves and robbers may bar your way
And may attack you night and day.
If you don't dwell in a good land,
How can you live well and well stand?
A bit can the big explicate;
A household is just like a state.
Chough and Ch'in guarded by Case Dale
Were well fortified without fail.
One thrived for four hundred years on;

>   The other perished, far off gone.
>   I've a word for you, house or state:
>   It's men who're bad, not the estate.

* Long Peace: Ch'ang'an if transliterated, the metropolis of gold, the capital of the T'ang Empire, with 1,000,000 inhabitants, the largest walled city ever built by man, and now the capital of today's Sha'anhsi Province. Long Peace saw the wonder of Chinese civilization that reached the pinnacle of brilliance in Emperor Deepsire's reign.
* pine: any of a genus (*Pinus*) of evergreen trees of the pine family, a cone-bearing tree having bundles of two to five needle-shaped leaves growing in clusters, an important image in Chinese literature, a symbol of rectitude, longevity and so on.
* owl: a predatory nocturnal bird, having large eyes and head, short, sharply hooked bill, long powerful claws, and a circular facial disk of radiating feathers, regarded as ominous in Chinese culture.
* orchid: any of a widely distributed family of terrestrial or epiphytic monocotyledonous plants having thickened bulbous roots and often very showy distinctive flowers, one of the four most important floral images in Chinese literature, which are wintersweet, orchid, bamboo, and chrysanthemum.
* fox: a burrowing canine mammal (genus *Vulpes*) having a long pointed muzzle and a long bushy tail, commonly reddish-brown in color, characterized by its cunning.
* Pa: an ancient state, an area covering present-day Double Gain (Ch'ungch'ing), the east of Ssuch'uan, the west of Hupei, and north of Kuichow and the northwest of Hunan.
* Yung: an ancient state in today's Mt. Bamboo, Hupei Province, conquered by Ch'u in the Spring and Autumn period.
* rat: any of numerous long tailed rodents of various families resembling but larger than the mouse. In some cases, rats are very destructive pests or carriers of highly contagious diseases, as bubonic plague and typhus.
* snake: an ophidian reptile, having a greatly elongated, scaly body, no limbs, and a specialized swallowing apparatus, a symbol of indifference, malevolence, cattiness, and craftiness in Chinese culture.
* Chough: the State of Chough (1046 B.C. – 256 B.C.), the third kingdom in Chinese history, comprising Western Chough and Eastern Chough.
* Ch'in: the Ch'in State or the State of Ch'in (905 B.C.– 206 B.C.), enfeoffed as a dependency of Chough by King Piety of Chough in 905 B.C. and enfeoffed as a vassal state by King Peace of Chough in 770 B.C. In the ten years from 230 B.C. to 221 B.C.,

Ch'in wiped out the other six powers and became the first unified regime of China, i.e., the Ch'in Empire.

* Case Dale: Case Dale Pass — an ancient pass located to the east of Long Peace, the capital of the T'ang Empire, and Lint'ao, a noted county was to the west.

有木诗八首
Eight Poems of Plants

其 一

有木名弱柳，
结根近清池。
风烟借颜色，
雨露助华滋。
峨峨白雪花，
袅袅青丝枝。
渐密阴自庇，
转高梢四垂。
截枝扶为杖，
软弱不自持。
折条用樊圃，
柔脆非其宜。
为树信可玩，
论材何所施。
可惜金堤地，
栽之徒尔为。

No. 1

There's a plant that is willow called,
Rooted by the side of a pool.
Wind and mist touches it with hue;
It grows lush, winds fine and dews cool.
Its catkins fly there like white snow;

Its greenish sprays put forth and out.
When leaves are dense, a shade is cast;
Its top reaches high to spread about.
Its branch is cut to make a cane,
But too soft, it can't self-sustain.
Its twigs are picked to make a fence,
But too crisp, they can't long remain.
As a tree, it's where one can play;
As timber, it's of no use there.
What a pity, the gold sand dyke,
Has it for nothing, not a hair.

* willow: any of a large genus of shrubs and trees related to the poplars, having generally smooth branches, and often long, slender, pliant, and sometimes pendent branchlets, a symbol of farewell or nostalgia in Chinese culture.
* catkin: a deciduous scaly spike of flowers, as in the willow, an image of helpless drifting or wandering in Chinese literature.

其 二

有木名樱桃,
得地早滋茂。
叶密独承日,
花繁偏受露。
迎风暗摇动,
引鸟潜来去。
鸟啄子难成,
风来枝莫住。
低软易攀玩,
佳人屡回顾。
色求桃李饶,
心向松筠妒。
好是映墙花,
本非当轩树。
所以姓萧人,
曾为伐樱赋。

No. 2

There's a plant that is cherry called;
Roots in the soil, it grows with hue.
Its thick leaves keep one from the sun;
Its dense flowers take in morning dew.
In wind it flutters up and down,
Luring birds to fly to and fro.
Pecked by them, fruit can hardly be;
Its twigs sway when wind starts to blow.
Low and soft, it's easy to climb;

Beauties often look back to shine;
Its colors outshine peach and plum,
So envied by bamboo and pine.
It just provides flowers for the wall,
Not timber for carts to be made.
So there was a man, Hsiao by name
Once wrote a cherry serenade.

* cherry: any of various trees (genus *Prunus*) of the rose family, related to the plum and the peach and bearing small, round or heart-shaped drupes enclosing a smooth pit; especially the sweet cherry, the sour cherry and the wild black cherry.
* peach: any of the plant (*Prunus Percica*), bearing a fleshy, juicy, edible drupe, cultivated in many varieties in temperate zones, considered sacred in China, a symbol of romance, prosperity and longevity.
* plum: a kind of plant or the edible purple drupaceous fruit of the plant which is any one of various trees of the genus *Prunus*, cultivated in temperate zones.
* bamboo: a tall, tree-like or shrubby grass in tropical and semi-tropical regions, a symbol of integrity and altitude, one of the four most important botanical images in Chinese literature, which are wintersweet, orchid, bamboo, and chrysanthemum. Bamboo shoots, fresh or dried, are widely used in Chinese cuisine, bamboo rats and bamboo worms are regarded as table delicacies.
* pine: any of a genus (*Pinus*) of evergreen trees of the pine family, a cone-bearing tree having bundles of two to five needle-shaped leaves growing in clusters, an important image in Chinese literature, a symbol of rectitude, longevity and so on.

其 三

有木秋不凋,
青青在江北。
谓为洞庭橘,
美人自移植。
上受顾昕恩,
下勤浇溉力。
实成乃是枳,
臭苦不堪食。
物有似是者,
真伪何由识。
美人默无言,
对之长叹息。
中含害物意,
外矫凌霜色。
仍向枝叶间,
潜生刺如棘。

No. 3

There's a tree whose leaves do not fall,
On the northern bank growing green.
Someone calls it Cavehall orange;
A man transplants it for fruit sheen.
He, like blessed with power from above,
Waters and manures it, all raised.
It bears no ranges but pulp bulbs,
With a bad smell and a sour taste;
A thing may look good from the skin;

How can we really know it's good.
The planter does not say a word,
He heaves a sigh from his bad mood.
It contains some toxin inside,
Having a shining face to show.
Its leaves conceal prickles and thorns
While thickly and densely they grow.

* Cavehall: Lake Cavehall, a large lake with an area of 2,740 square kilometers, a lake of strategic importance since ancient times, a place of many resources for today's Hunan Province.
* orange: a reddish, yellow, round, edible citrus fruit, with a sweet, juicy pulp; any of various evergreen trees (genus *Citrus*) of the rue family bearing this fruit.

其 四

有木名杜梨,
阴森覆丘壑。
心蠹已空朽,
根深尚盘薄。
狐媚言语巧,
妖鸟声音恶。
凭此为巢穴,
往来互栖托。
四傍五六本,
叶枝相交错。
借问因何生,
秋风吹子落。
为长社坛下,
无人敢芟斫。
几度野火来,
风回烧不着。

No. 4

There's a tree birchleaf pear by name,
Whose shade is cast down to the dale.
Its trunk has been rotten with bugs;
Its roots down in the soil prevail.
Foxes play their sweet eyes and tongues;
Owls utter cries so sharp and coarse.
They build their nests upon the boughs
And perch in them as their recourse.
Five or six boughs each other help,

With twigs and leaves entwined and bound.
Why does this tree in this world grow?
The wind blow seeds to fall aground.
No one dare cut it or chop it,
As it is worshiped in the shrine.
A few times fires have come along,
But they can't reach it, bad or fine.

* birchleaf pear: *Pyrus calleryana Decne*, a perennial tree, having white flowers and brown or reddish fruit.
* fox: a burrowing canine mammal (genus *Vulpes*) having a long pointed muzzle and a long bushy tail, commonly reddish-brown in color, characterized by its cunning.
* owl: a predatory nocturnal bird, having large eyes and head, short, sharply hooked bill, long powerful claws, and a circular facial disk of radiating feathers, regarded as ominous in Chinese culture.

其　五

有木香苒苒，
山头生一麓。
主人不知名，
移种近轩闼。
爱其有芳味，
因以调麹蘖。
前后曾饮者，
十人无一活。
岂徒悔封植，
兼亦误采掇。
试问识药人，
始知名野葛。
年深已滋蔓，
刀斧不可伐。
何时猛风来，
为我连根拔。

No. 5

There's a tree giving off perfume
Which wafts o'er the hills without aim;
It's transplanted beside the door
Of a man who knows not its name.
He loves its smell and pulls it out
And puts it into his wine pot;
Of ten men having drunk the wine,
All are dead now, surviving not.
One should regret having grown it

And having concocted the wine.
He asks one who knows medicine
And comes to know it's wild bean vine.
It's so strong as it's grown so long;
That no axe can fell it at all.
When will we have a high wind here
To uproot it and make it fall.

其 六

有木名水柽，
远望青童童。
根株非劲挺，
柯叶多蒙笼。
彩翠色如柏，
鳞皴皮似松。
为同松柏类，
得列嘉树中。
枝弱不胜雪，
势高常惧风。
雪压低还举，
风吹西复东。
柔芳甚杨柳，
早落先梧桐。
惟有一堪赏，
中心无蠹虫。

No. 6

There's a tree tamarisk by name;
That's green if from afar you gaze.
Its roots or trunk not so upright,
Its leaves are thick, looking like haze.
Its emerald looks like a cypress;
Its scaled bark looks like an old pine.
Of pines and cypresses, this kind,
It belongs to trees we call fine.
Its weakling twigs cannot stand snow;

On high, by wind it's often pressed.
Pressed down by snow, it stands as e'er;
While wind blows now east and then west.
It's softer than a willow tree;
Earlier than scholar trees its leaves fall.
There's one thing that we can admire:
In its truck there's no bug at all.

* tamarisk: any of a small genus of small trees or shrubs of the tamarisk family with slender branches and feathery flowery clusters, common near salt water and often grown for windbreak.
* pine: any of a genus (*Pinus*) of evergreen trees of the pine family, a cone-bearing tree having bundles of two to five needle-shaped leaves growing in clusters, an important image in Chinese literature, a symbol of rectitude, longevity and so on.
* cypress: an evergreen tree of the family Cupressaceae, having durable timber, a symbol of rectitude, nobility and longevity in Chinese culture.

其 七

有木名凌霄，
擢秀非孤标。
偶依一株树，
遂抽百尺条。
托根附树身，
开花寄树梢。
自谓得其势，
无因有动摇。
一旦树摧倒，
独立暂飘飖。
疾风从东起，
吹折不终朝。
朝为拂云花，
暮为委地樵。
寄言立身者，
勿学柔弱苗。

No. 7

There's a tree there campsis by name,
Growing tall, delicate, and fair.
It happens to lean on a trunk,
With a hundred-feet-long vines there.
With its roots encircling the trunk,
It bursts into blossoms ablaze.
It has a predominant place,
Not because over there it sways.
Once the trunk it leans on falls down,

Hanging, flowing, it does suspend.
A strong wind rises from the east,
And blows, punching it without end.
In the morning its flowers stroke clouds;
At dusk it falls aground as wood.
Those who'd be established I urge,
Don't be a weak vine if you could.

* campsis: Campsis grandiflora, a deciduous creeping vine, having pinnate compound leaves and orange-red flower clusters.

其 八

有木名丹桂，
四时香馥馥。
花团夜雪明，
叶剪春云绿。
风影清似水，
霜枝冷如玉。
独占小山幽，
不容凡鸟宿。
匠人爱芳直，
裁截为厦屋。
干细力未成，
用之君自速。
重任虽大过，
直心终不曲。
纵非梁栋材，
犹胜寻常木。

No. 8

There's a tree osmanthus by name,
Which gives off perfume all year round.
Covered with moonlit snow at night;
To put forth leaves green it's bound.
Its cool shade is clean, water-like;
Its frosted twigs are like jade best.
It occupies a quiet small hill
Where no wrens can build their nest.
A master loves its balmy wood,

And cuts it to build a cool hut.
Please make use of the wood right now
Before into fine bits it's cut.
Though one can expect much of it,
It's so frank as a good resource.
Though it's not enough as a beam,
It outdoes common wood, of course.

* osmanthus: any plant of the genus *Osmanthus Lur.*, native to Asia and America, having fragrant small yellow or yellow-whitish flowers.
* wren: any of numerous small passerine birds, having short rounded wings and a short tail, symbolizing something unimportant.

寓意诗五首
Five Allegorical Poems

其 一

豫樟生深山,
七年而后知。
挺高二百尺,
本末皆十围。
天子建明堂,
此材独中规。
匠人执斤墨,
采度将有期。
孟冬草木枯,
烈火燎山陂。
疾风吹猛焰,
从根烧到枝。
养材三十年,
方成栋梁姿。
一朝为灰烬,
柯叶无孑遗。
地虽生尔材,
天不与尔时。
不如粪上英,
犹有人掇之。
已矣勿重陈,
重陈令人悲。
不悲焚烧苦,
但悲采用迟。

No. 1

A camphor in high mountains grows;
After seven years it is found.
Growing majestic with a trunk
As thick as ten armfuls around.
The Most High would build a bright hall;
It's the best timber to fit well.
Carpenters have come and surveyed
And fixed the date the tree they'll fell.
A mad fire breaks out on the slope,
As winter sees plants and grass dry.
The tree is burned from root to top,
As wind-fanned fire licks far and nigh.
For thirty years it has grown big
To be good timber size and heft.
So soon it has turned into ash,
Until no twig or leaf is left.
Although the good earth brought you up,
Heaven does not give you much luck.
You can't compare with flowers on dung
Which somebody will come to pluck.
Don't talk about it any more,
Or our hearts will fall down to cry.
We don't cry for the burning pain,
But over the missed chance we sigh.

* camphor: camphor tree, a large evergreen tree of Eastern Asia yielding the camphor of commerce.

其 二

赫赫京内史，
炎炎中书郎。
昨传征拜日，
恩赐颇殊常。
貂冠水苍玉，
紫绶黄金章。
佩服身未暖，
已闻窜遐荒。
亲戚不得别，
吞声泣路旁。
宾客亦已散，
门前雀罗张。
富贵来不久，
倏如瓦沟霜。
权势去尤速，
瞥若石火光。
不如守贫贱，
贫贱可久长。
传语宦游子，
且来归故乡。

No. 2

The Mayor of Long Peace so great,
The secretariat in great power.
They were appointed yesterday;
Grants and honors fall like a shower.
They're granted sable hats and jade;

Purple sashes, gold seals so dear.
These not yet warming their bodies,
They were banished to the frontier.
Their dear ones dare not bid good-bye,
Standing crying there by the way.
Their guests and friends being dispersed
Before their doors all sparrows play.
Wealth and ranks rush to them so fast,
Like frost falling upon their tiles.
Their power goes away all too soon,
Like flint glints for sporadic whiles.
We'd better in poverty stay;
In poverty, we can long last.
All those in office far away,
Do come back home, do come back fast.

* Long Peace: referring to Ch'ang'an if transliterated, the metropolis of gold, the capital of the T'ang, the largest walled city ever built by man.
* sparrow: a small, plain-colored passerine bird related to the finches, grosbeaks and buntings, a very common bird in China, a symbol of insignificance.

其 三

促织不成章，
提壶但闻声。
嗟哉虫与鸟，
无实有虚名。
与君定交日，
久要如弟兄。
何以示诚信，
白水指为盟。
云雨一为别，
飞沉两难并。
君为得风鹏，
我为失水鲸。
音信日已疏，
恩分日已轻。
穷通尚如此，
何况死与生。
乃知择交难，
须有知人明。
莫将山上松，
结托水上萍。

No. 3

The crickets cheep, cheep now and then,
Which I hear, carrying my pot.
Why and my, all insects and birds;
They are all vain, real they are not.
Now we have become friends today;

For life best brothers we shall be.
How to prove we're sincere and true?
The white water's our oath we'll see.
Now we're apart like cloud and rain
You're flying high and I will land.
You're the roc soaring before wind,
And I'm a whale bumping astrand.
As time goes by letters are few;
Long divided, grace starts to fall.
To rise and fall is just like this,
Let alone death and life for all.
If you know making friends is hard,
One's integrity you should note.
Be a staunch pine atop the hill
Instead of duckweed there afloat.

* cricket: a leaping orthopterans insect, with long antennae and three segments in each tarsus, the male of which makes a chirping sound by friction of forewings, a common image of a quiet night in Chinese literature.
* roc: a legendary enormous powerful bird of prey. In Chinese mythology, it was transformed from a fish in North Sea. *Sir Lush* reads like this: there in North Sea is a fish called Minnow, whose body spans about a thousand miles. When transformed into a bird, it is called Roc, whose back spans about a thousand miles. With a burst of vigor, it flies up, whose wings are like clouds hemming the sky. This bird, skimming tides, flies to South Sea. And this South Sea is called the Pool of Heaven.
* whale: a giant cetaceous mammal of fish-like form, especially one of the larger pelagic species, as distinguished from dolphins and porpoises. Whales have the fore limbs developed as broad flattened paddles, hind limbs degenerated, and a thick layer of fat or blubber immediately beneath the skin. A whale is a symbol of great ambition, fortitude and uniqueness.
* pine: a cone-bearing evergreen tree having needle-shaped leaves growing in clusters, a symbol of rectitude, fortitude and longevity in Chinese culture.
* duckweed: any of several small, disk-shaped, floating aquatic plants common in streams and ponds.

其　四

翩翩两玄鸟，
本是同巢燕。
分飞来几时，
秋夏炎凉变。
一宿蓬荜庐，
一栖明光殿。
偶因衔泥处，
复得重相见。
彼矜杏梁贵，
此嗟茅栋贱。
眼看秋社至，
两处俱难恋。
所托各暂时，
胡为相叹羡。

No. 4

Two black birds take wings to fly high;
Once, they were swallows in the nest.
Apart they have flown for so long,
In summer raised, in autumn pressed.
One lives in a bright palace hall,
Another dwells by a thatched lane.
Once they come out to peck for mud,
And each other they see again.
One sighs the apricot beam's dear,
The other blame the thatched roof's cheap.
Now autumn sacrifice gets near;

Afar they can't together keep.
For the time being they are laid by
Then why do you each to each cry.

* swallow: a passerine black bird, with short broad, depressed bill, long pointed wings, and forked tail, noted for fleeting flight and migratory habits. In Chinese culture, swallows are welcome to live with a family with their nests on a beam.
* apricot: a tree or the fruit of the tree of the rose family, intermediate between the peach and the plum. Growing, reaping or selling apricots alludes to a hermit who is kind to the folks, just like Feng Tung, who gave free medical treatment to them except that he asked them to plant one to five apricot trees for him according to the severity of their illness.

其 五

婆娑园中树，
根株大合围。
蠢尔树间虫，
形质一何微。
孰谓虫之微，
蛊蠹已无期。
孰谓树之大，
花叶有衰时。
花衰夏未实，
叶病秋先萎。
树心半为土，
观者安得知。
借问虫何在，
在身不在枝。
借问虫何食，
食心不食皮。
岂无啄木鸟，
觜长将何为？

No. 5

There dance the leaves of a court tree,
Its trunk an armful, a tree tall.
The foolish bugs upon the leaves
Wriggle, wriggle, looking so small.
Who says the bugs there are so small?
They are all there year after year.
Who says the tree there is so tall?

Its flowers and leaves are bound to sear.
The flowers wither, fruit not yet born
The leaves so sick in autumn flow.
The trunk is half wood, and half dirt;
About this, does a viewer know?
Please let me know where the bugs are;
In the trunk, not in the twigs, o dear.
Please let me know what the bug eat?
The heart, not the bark, as is clear.
Hark, the woodpecker does there coo;
With its long bill what does it do?

* woodpecker: any of a large family of birds related to the flickers, having stiff tail feathers to aid in climbing, strong claws, and a sharp, chisel-like bill for drilling holes in wood in search of insects.

秦中吟十首(选三)

Chants in Long Peace (Three Poems Out of Ten)

贞元、元和之际,予在长安,闻见之间,有足悲者。因直歌其事,命为《秦中吟》。

During the reigns of Right One and One Cord, I am in Long Peace, viewing and hearing things that perturb me, so I write about them and name the poems *Chants in Long Peace*.

议　婚

天下无正声,
悦耳即为娱。
人间无正色,
悦目即为姝。
颜色非相远,
贫富则有殊。
贫为时所弃,
富为时所趋。
红楼富家女,
金缕绣罗襦。
见人不敛手,
娇痴二八初。
母兄未开口,
已嫁不须臾。
绿窗贫家女,
寂寞二十馀。
荆钗不直钱,
衣上无真珠。

几回人欲聘，
临日又踟蹰。
主人会良媒，
置酒满玉壶。
四座且勿饮，
听我歌两途。
富家女易嫁，
嫁早轻其夫。
贫家女难嫁，
嫁晚孝于姑。
闻君欲娶妇，
娶妇意何如？

Marriage

No pure right tune there is on earth;
Pleasant to the ear, it's of worth.
No pure right girl there is to dwell;
Pleasant to the eye, she's the belle.
In looks, difference there is no much;
In wealth, difference is huge as such.
When you are poor, all do you spurn;
When you are rich, to you all turn.
The rich daughter in the red tower
Has gold strings and silk robes as dower.
She restrains herself not when seen;
Spoilt and naive, she's but sixteen.
Before her parents start to say,
She's married away right away.
A poor daughter in her green room
Has been there twenty years in gloom.

Her hairpin is cheap on her hair,
And has no real jewels to wear.
To propose, a few come their way,
But they hesitate on the day.
A match-maker knows the whole lot;
She waits for wine to fill the pot.
"Lay down your cups, all of you here;
Before you drink, lend me your ear."
Rich girls go marry with delight;
So early, their husband they slight.
Poor girls go marry with all pain;
Although late, their house they sustain.
I hear you will soon wed a wife,
But what does that mean to your life?

重 赋

厚地植桑麻，
所要济生民。
生民理布帛，
所求活一身。
身外充征赋，
上以奉君亲。
国家定两税，
本意在忧人。
厥初防其淫，
明敕内外臣：
税外加一物，
皆以枉法论。
奈何岁月久，
贪吏得因循。
浚我以求宠，
敛索无冬春。
织绢未成匹，
缲丝未盈斤。
里胥迫我纳，
不许暂逡巡。
岁暮天地闭，
阴风生破村。
夜深烟火尽，
霰雪白纷纷。
幼者形不蔽，
老者体无温。
悲端与寒气，
并入鼻中辛。

昨日输残税，
因窥官库门：
缯帛如山积，
丝絮似云屯。
号为羡馀物，
随月献至尊。
夺我身上暖，
买尔眼前恩。
进入琼林库，
岁久化为尘！

Heavy Tax

Mulberries and hemp in the field
Meet the need of folks with the yield.
The folks grow and weave night and day
To sustain themselves while they may.
Except necessities, that sort,
They give all they have to the court.
Two taxes laid down by the state
Were to folks' burden alleviate.
At first strict measures were taken
To tax more all were forbidden.
If an official would add more,
It was a grave breach of the law.
Howe'er, as days and months flew by,
Corrupt officials went awry.
For their riches, honors and power,
They taxed the folks to seek the hour.
Cloth, not yet a roll did they yield!
Silk, not yet a catty was reeled!

The village head pressed me to pay:
"No hesitation, right away!"
The year was gone, sky and earth furled;
Chilly wind to the village whirled.
At night, smoke and fire dying out;
Flurry and snow flying about.
Children in tatters poor and old;
The old folks shivering with cold.
Indignation and the cold spell
Became pains too severe to tell.
To make up the tax yesterday,
In Grand Barn he saw what there lay.
Silks and textiles were piled so high,
Like thick clouds above in the sky.
Surplus of store is what they call,
Therewith they'd buy favor, buy all.
You rob me of all my supplies
To buy the grace before your eyes.
Once you tribute them to the crown,
They will decay, like soil pressed down.

* mulberry: the edible, berry-like fruit of a tree (genus *Morus*) whose leaves are valued for silkworm culture, and the tree itself, first cultivated in the drainage area of the Yellow River in China about five thousand years ago.
* hemp: a tall annual Asian herb (*Gannabis sativa*) of the mulberry family, with small green flowers and a tough bark, the fibers from which are used for cloth and cordage.
* silk: the fine, soft, shiny fiber produced by silk worms to form their cocoons, and the thread or fabric made from this fibre is used as material for clothing. And it can be any clothing made of silk.

买　花

帝城春欲暮，
喧喧车马度。
共道牡丹时，
相随买花去。
贵贱无常价，
酬直看花数。
灼灼百朵红，
戋戋五束素。
上张幄幕庇，
旁织巴篱护。
水洒复泥封，
移来色如故。
家家习为俗，
人人迷不悟。
有一田舍翁，
偶来买花处。
低头独长叹，
此叹无人喻。
一丛深色花，
十户中人赋。

Buying Flowers

Capital sees the end of spring;
Carts and horses too much noise bring.
All praise peonies at their best hours;
Why not go now to buy the flowers?
Good or poor, they have no fixed price;

When paying you look twice and thrice.
Ablaze, ablaze, a hundred bright;
Quite few, quite few, five bundles white.
In a hood they are kept so well;
With a hedge, safety one can tell.
Watered and their roots sealed with clay,
So moved, their colors as e'er stay.
Each household take them as they are;
Each person loves them all too far.
There is an old farmer o'er there,
Who sometimes comes to the flower fair.
His head bent, he heaves a long sigh;
Of his sigh, nobody knows why.
For a cluster of flowers real gay,
Ten households' taxes for the pay.

* peony: any of a genus of perennial, often double-flowered, plants of the peony family, with large pink, yellow, red, or white showy flowers, cultivated as early as the Sui dynasty in China, became popular in the T'ang dynasty and well-known in the Sung dynasty. The best peonies are those cultivated in Loshine.

续古诗十首
Ten Old Poems

其 一

戚戚复戚戚，
送君远行役。
行役非中原，
海外黄沙碛。
伶俜独居妾，
迢递长征客。
君望功名归，
妾忧生死隔。
谁家无夫妇，
何人不离坼。
所恨薄命身，
嫁迟别日迫。
妾身有存殁，
妾心无改易。
生作闺中妇，
死作山头石。

No. 1

Sad and so sad, what pain and pain,
She sees off her husband afar.
Seeing him not to the mid-plain,
But to the seashore where sands are.
So poor, I keep my room alone

He is on the march, far apart.
May he make great success, well-known;
Still, I'm worried, so keen, so smart.
Which man goes on without a mate?
Which wife does not in quietude stay?
But I'm aggrieved much at my fate;
I was wed so briefly that day.
E'en though I'm buried in my tomb,
I'll live up to my faith for aye.
Alive, for him I'll keep the room,
And I'll be a rock when I die.

其 二

掩泪别乡里,
飘飘将远行。
茫茫绿野中,
春尽孤客情。
驱马上丘陇,
高低路不平。
风吹棠梨花,
啼鸟时一声。
古墓何代人,
不知姓与名。
化作路傍土,
年年春草生。
感彼忽自悟,
今我何营营。

No. 2

Brushing my tears I leave my town,
Far, far away like thistledown.
Like lost in the wilderness green,
The spring gone I'm lonely, I'm keen.
I gallop up a sloppy hill;
The bumpy trail dampens my will.
A wind does cherry blossoms sweep
And starts out of a bird a cheep.
Who's in the grave, a-lying there?
I do not know his name, whate'er.
He has become dirt by the trail,

Year in, year out, grass does prevail.
I ask myself: "What will I do?
And what will my toil amount to?"

* thistledown: the pappus of a thistle, a kind of vigorous prickly plant with cylindrical or globular heads of tubular purple flowers, an important image in Chinese Literature, a symbol of helpless vagrancy or straying.
* cherry: any of various trees (genus *Prunus*) of the rose family, related to the plum and the peach and bearing small, round or heart-shaped drupes enclosing a smooth pit; especially the sweet cherry, the sour cherry and the wild black cherry.

其 三

朝采山上薇，
暮采山上薇。
岁晏薇亦尽，
饥来何所为。
坐饮白石水，
手把青松枝。
击节独长歌，
其声清且悲。
枥马非不肥，
所苦常絷维。
豢豕非不饱，
所忧竟为牺。
行行歌此曲，
以慰常苦饥。

No. 3

At dawn I gather ferns uphill;
At dusk I gather ferns uphill.
The year's going to disappear;
How could I bear hunger severe?
I sit drinking from the white stone,
Holding a pine twig greenly grown.
Knocking the trunk I sing aloud
And sing towards the fleecy cloud.
It's not that my horse is not fat,
But that it is kept in like that.
It's not that my pig is not fed,

　　　　　But that it's sacrificed instead.
　　　　　I go on and on, and I sing
　　　　　To stop my hunger and my sting.

* fern: any of a widely distributed class of flowerless, seedless pteridophytic plants, having roots and stems and feathery leaves (fronds) which carry the reproductive spores in clusters of sporangia called sori. Its young stems and root starch are table delicacies to Chinese now as well as in the past.
* pine: any of a genus (*Pinus*) of evergreen trees of the pine family, a cone-bearing tree having bundles of two to five needle-shaped leaves growing in clusters, an important image in Chinese literature, a symbol of rectitude, longevity and so on.

其 四

雨露长纤草，
山苗高入云。
风雪折劲木，
涧松摧为薪。
风摧此何意？
雨长彼何因？
百丈涧底死，
寸茎山上春。
可怜苦节士，
感此涕盈巾。

No. 4

With rain and dew thin grass does grow;
The saplings on the hill reach the blue.
In wind and snow there break trees tall;
The creek pines as firewood do fall.
Why does the wind blow to the top?
Why does the rain swish without stop?
Trees die in dales miles and miles deep;
Grass spreads on slopes abruptly steep.
Scholars so bitter, with all pain,
Your sad tears your turbans will stain.

---

* pine: any of a genus (*Pinus*) of evergreen trees of the pine family, a cone-bearing tree having bundles of two to five needle-shaped leaves growing in clusters, an important image in Chinese literature, a symbol of rectitude, longevity and so on.

其　五

窈窕双鬟女，
容德俱如玉。
昼居不逾阈，
夜行常秉烛。
气如含露兰，
心如贯霜竹。
宜当备嫔御，
胡为守幽独。
无媒不得选，
年忽过三六。
岁暮望汉宫，
谁在黄金屋。
邯郸进倡女，
能唱黄花曲。
一曲称君心，
恩荣连九族。

No. 5

So slender, the double-bunned maid,
Her face and virtue both like jade.
At day time indoors she stays;
At night the candle to her rays.
Like orchids, she does brightly sheen;
Like bamboo, her heart is so clean.
She should be one serving the throne;
Why should she stay in all alone?
She won't wed with no go-between;

After this year, she'll be eighteen.
There the palace she does behold;
Year gone, who's in the house of gold?
Hantan folks send girls to the court
So as to sing *Yellow Flowers* fine.
If a maid can the crown disport,
Hers will be honored for ages nine.

* orchid: any of a widely distributed family of terrestrial or epiphytic monocotyledonous plants having thickened bulbous roots and often very showy distinctive flowers, one of the four most important floral images in Chinese literature, which are wintersweet, orchid, bamboo, and chrysanthemum.
* bamboo: a tall, tree-like or shrubby grass in tropical and semi-tropical regions, a symbol of integrity and altitude, one of the four most important images in Chinese literature, which are wintersweet, orchid, bamboo, and chrysanthemum.
* Hantan: a city more than 3,100 years old, the capital of the State of Chao (403 B.C.- 222 B.C.) in the Eastern Chough dynasty (770 B.C.- 256 B.C.), located in present-day Hopei Province. This city was built in the Shang dynasty (cir. 1600 B.C.- cir. 1046 B.C.) and an imperial palace was built here for King Chow (cir. 1105 B.C.- 1046 B.C.) according to *Lonely Bamboo Annals*. The legacies and ruins bespeak the splendor of its glorious past.

其 六

栖栖远方士，
读书三十年。
业成无知己，
徒步来入关。
长安多王侯，
英俊竞攀援。
幸随众宾末，
得厕门馆间。
东阁有旨酒，
中堂有管弦。
何为向隅客，
对此不开颜。
富贵无是非，
主人终日欢。
贫贱多悔尤，
客子中夜叹。
归去复归去，
故乡贫亦安。

No. 6

A scholar comes here from afar;
For thirty years he has now read.
To him no bosom friends there are;
To the capital he does tread.
Long Peace boasts many, many peers,
Who try hard to climb up and soar.
He follows them close in the rears

And comes to a hall through a door.
In East Wing a feast's going on,
The strings played in the central room.
Why of the guests should I be one
Crest-fallen, and failing in gloom?
So rich and high, they have the power;
All day long seeking their delight.
Those poor and low worry each hour
And I sigh in the depth of night.
Go back to my town, go back to my town;
Though it's poor, I can settle down.

* Long Peace: Ch'ang'an if transliterated, the capital of the T'ang Empire, with 1,000,000 inhabitants, the largest walled city ever built by man.
* East Wing: a hall in the palace.

其 七

凉风飘嘉树，
日夜减芳华。
下有感秋妇，
攀条苦悲嗟。
我本幽闲女，
结发事豪家。
豪家多婢仆，
门内颇骄奢。
良人近封侯，
出入鸣玉珂。
自从富贵来，
恩薄谗言多。
冢妇独守礼，
群妾互奇邪。
但信言有玷，
不察心无瑕。
容光未销歇，
欢爱忽蹉跎。
何意掌上玉，
化为眼中砂。
盈盈一尺水，
浩浩千丈河。
勿言小大异，
随分有风波。
闺房犹复尔，
邦国当如何。

No. 7

The chill wind blows to the fine trees;
Day and night its prime does decrease.
A woman in autumn there sighs
While the foliage bitterly cries.
I'm a girl who once lived in peace
But was married to the rich gate.
There so many servants one sees
And my husband feels proudly great.
He does seem like one of the peer;
As he walks on, his pendants clink.
Since I joined the family here,
Mouths evil spat, eyes wicked wink.
Alone, to the rite I keep close;
His concubines so evil be.
He does think my speech amiss goes;
My heart flawless he does not see.
Before the colors of mine fade;
His love and romance passes by.
On his palm I was once his jade;
Now I'm but a grit in his eye.
A pond of water is so small;
A surging river is so wide.
Don't say they're just different at all;
When wind blows, there will be a tide.
If a household could go amiss,
Doesn't a state just run like this?

* jade: a variety of translucent precious stone, exclusive to the upper echelon of the

society in ancient China, but gold and silver are not, as a saying goes, "Gold is priced while jade is priceless." It is used as a metaphor for something good or rare, like jade pot, jade steps, Jade Mirror Pool, Jade Maid, even Jade Emperor.

其 八

心亦无所迫，
身亦无所拘。
何为肠中气，
郁郁不得舒。
不舒良有以，
同心久离居。
五年不见面，
三年不得书。
念此令人老，
抱膝坐长吁。
岂无盈尊酒，
非君谁与娱。

No. 8

My heart does no coercion bear,
And my body's totally free.
Why in my bowels stagnant is air,
So that relieved I cannot be?
Long have I been sickly like this,
For we haven't had rains and dews.
For five years gone, my man I miss;
For three years from him there's no news.
For this I'm getting old, I pine;
For long I sigh, hugging my knees.
Where can I get a cup of wine?
But without you, who can me please?

* three years: it may not be exactly three years, but is used in a vague sense of a long period of time.

其 九

揽衣出门行，
游观绕林渠。
澹澹春水暖，
东风生绿蒲。
上有和鸣雁，
下有掉尾鱼。
飞沉一何乐，
鳞羽各有徒。
而我方独处，
不与之子俱。
顾彼自伤己，
禽鱼之不如。
出游欲遣忧，
孰知忧有馀。

No. 9

My clothes in arms, outside I go;
Around the wooded trench I walk.
Undulating, a stream does flow;
For spring wind the sedge sways its stalk.
Singing above, there fly wild geese;
Playing below, there chase small fish.
Flying or swimming, they're at ease;
Each kind has each kind's fun or wish.
In solitude I sit nearby;
Why the hell can't I stay with her?
Looking afar, for long I sigh;

The birds and fish do my heart stir.
Strolling outside, I'd my cure sore;
Who knows my sore hurts all the more?

* sedge: a grasslike cyperaceous herb with flowers densely clustered in spikes and widely distributed in marshy places.
* wild goose: an undomesticated goose that is caring and responsible, taken as a symbol of benevolence, righteousness, good manner, wisdom, and faith in Chinese culture.

其 十

春旦日初出，
瞳瞳耀晨辉。
草木照未远，
浮云已蔽之。
天地黯以晦，
当午如昏时。
虽有东南风，
力微不能吹。
中园何所有，
满地青青葵。
阳光委云上，
倾心欲何依。

No. 10

At spring dawn the new sun shines bright
And spreads morning glow far and wide.
Before plants and grass enjoy light，
Clouds float gather and do it hide.
Sky and earth are dark，with no glow
It seems like night，though it is noon.
Although an east wind does here blow，
It's so weak，and vanishes soon.
What's there in the garden o'er there?
Green mallow covering the ground.
Over the clouds the sun does glare；
Where shall I go，where am I bound?

* mallow: a plant of the genus *Malva* with edible leaves, which was one of the five most popular vegetables in ancient China.

龙昌寺荷池

冷碧新秋水,
残红半破莲。
从来寥落意,
不似此池边。

The Lotus Pool at Dragonrise Temple

The failing lotus, fading red
In the autumn water so cool.
I sit alone, drooping my head,
Fallen like the flowers in the pool.

* Dragonrise Temple: an ancient temple in Loyal County in today's Ssuch'uan Province, comprising two temples, one uphill, the other downhill.
* lotus: one of the various plants of the waterlily family, characterized by their large floating round leaves and showy flowers, especially the white or pink Asian lotus, used as a religious symbol in Hinduism and Buddhism. In Chinese culture, it is a symbol of purity and elegance, unsoiled though out of soil, so clean with all leaves green. It is a common image in Chinese literature, as two lines of a lyric by Hsiu Ouyang (A.D. 1007 - A.D. 1072) read: "A thunder brings rain to the wood and pool, / The rain hushes the lotus, drips cool."

食　饱

食饱拂枕卧，
睡足起闲吟。
浅酌一杯酒，
缓弹数弄琴。
既可畅情性，
亦足傲光阴。
谁知利名尽，
无复长安心。

Well Fed

So fed, head on pillow I lie;
Sleep o'er, I rise to freely sing.
I drink a cup not filled so high
And slowly I finger a string.
Relaxed and relieved I can be,
So I can watch time slowly flow.
One should keep calm, of all cares free
To Long Peace no more need I go.

* Long Peace: Ch'ang'an if transliterated, the capital of the T'ang Empire, with 1,000,000 inhabitants, the largest walled city ever built by man. It's the capital of today's Sha'anhsi Province, with many cultural legacies, especially from the Han and the T'ang dynasties.

夜　雨

我有所念人，
隔在远远乡。
我有所感事，
结在深深肠。
乡远去不得，
无日不瞻望。
肠深解不得，
无夕不思量。
况此残灯夜，
独宿在空堂。
秋天殊未晓，
风雨正苍苍。
不学头陀法，
前心安可忘？

Night Rain

There is someone dearly I love,
But he's far away from the town.
There is something keenly I care,
And it's in my bowel, buried down.
The town so far, there I can't go;
Day after day, at there I gaze.
My bowel too deep, there I can't reach;
Night after night, my worry weighs.
Tonight by my tapering lamp,

I sit in my room all alone.
In this autumn when it's all dark,
The rain is by the wind hard blown.
If there's no Dhata in my mind,
How can I leave sad thoughts behind?

* Dhata: a manifestation as a controller of various attributes of human life, especially in the sense self-denial, mortification or asceticism.

邯郸冬至夜思家

邯郸驿里逢冬至，
抱膝灯前影伴身。
想得家中夜深坐，
还应说着远行人。

Thinking of Home on the Night of Winter Solstice in Hantan

In Hantan Post, I Winter Solstice passed;
I clasped my lit knees with my shadow cast.
I thought of my dear ones seated at night
Talking about me far away in plight.

* Hantan: the capital of Chao, a major city in today's Hopei Province. When threatened by the troops of Ch'in, Chao asked Faithridge for help. Hou suggested stealing the military tally, and Chu killed the commander with his gold hammer, so that Way's army was under Faithridge's command. In this way, Faithridge successfully saved Hantan.
* Winter Solstice: One of the 24 solar terms. Winter Solstice usually falls on December 22 or 23, when the daytime will be the shortest in a year. The twenty-four solar terms are listed as follows: Beginning of Spring (1st solar term), Rain Water (2nd solar term), Waking of Insects (3rd solar term), Spring Equinox (4th solar term), Pure Brightness (5th solar term), Grain Rain (6th solar term), Beginning of Summer (7th solar term), Grain Full (8th solar term), Grain in Ear (9th solar term), Summer Solstice (10th solar term), Slight Heat (11th solar term), Great Heat (12th solar term), Beginning of Autumn (13th solar term), Limit of Heat (14th solar term), White Dew (15th solar term), Autumnal Equinox (16th solar term), Cold Dew (17th solar term), Frost's Descent (18th solar term), Beginning

of Winter (19th solar term), Slight Snow (20th solar term), Great Snow (21st solar term), Winter Solstice (22nd solar term), Slight Cold (23rd solar term), and Great Cold (24th solar term).

赠　　内

生为同室亲,
死为同穴尘。
他人尚相勉,
而况我与君。
黔娄固穷士,
妻贤忘其贫。
冀缺一农夫,
妻敬俨如宾。
陶潜不营生,
翟氏自爨薪。
梁鸿不肯仕,
孟光甘布裙。
君虽不读书,
此事耳亦闻。
至此千载后,
传是何如人。
人生未死间,
不能忘其身。
所须者衣食,
不过饱与温。
蔬食足充饥,
何必膏粱珍。
缯絮足御寒,
何必锦绣文。
君家有贻训,
清白遗子孙。
我亦贞苦士,

与君新结婚。
庶保贫与素,
偕老同欣欣。

To My Wife

Alive, we two share the same room;
When dead, we lie in the same tomb.
In life, eye to eye others see,
Let alone the pair, you and me.
Dark Low would in hardship remain;
A good wife, you forget our pain.
Hope Lack, a farmer poor before;
His wife stood in respect and awe.
Ch'ien T'ao could not his house sustain;
Miss Ch'u managed all to maintain.
Swan Liang officialdom denied,
Light Meng would in plainness abide.
Though you don't read or know a word,
Of such stories you must have heard.
In one thousand years from today,
In our descendants' mind you'll stay.
So long as we live, live so far,
We should not forget who we are.
What we need is clothing and food;
Maintain ourselves well as we could.
Greens and grains are rather enough,
Why dainties, tidbits, all that stuff
Linen, cotton can fend off cold,
Why wear brocade, damask and gold?

You've learned family teachings good,
For our offspring's clean livelihood!
I, too, live a poor and hard life,
Newly married to you, my wife.
Let's live on, be simple and plain;
All life in gladness we'll remain.

* Dark Low: a hermit from Lu in the Spring and Autumn period, who died in poverty, e'en without enough clothing to cover his body.
* Hope Lack: a farmer from Chin in the Spring and Autumn period, living in poverty with love between husband and wife.
* Ch'ien T'ao: referring to Poolbright T'ao (A.D. 352 - A.D. 427), a verse writer, poet, and litterateur in the Chin dynasty, the founder of Chinese idyllism, and once the magistrate of P'engtse. He once lived in scarcity.
* Miss Ch'u: Ch'ien T'ao's wife, the third one, the former two having been dead.
* Swan Liang: a hermit and poet in the Eastern Han dynasty.
* Light Meng: Swan Liang's wife, who was respectful to her husband even if in poverty.
* cotton: the soft, white seed hairs filling the seedpods of various shrubby plants of the mallow family, originally native to the tropics, introduced to China in the Western Han dynasty.
* damask: a durable, lustrous, reversible fabric as of silk or linen, in figured weave, used for table linen, upholstery, etc.

寄　内

条桑初绿即为别，
柿叶半红犹未归。
不如村妇知时节，
解为田夫秋捣衣。

A Letter for My Wife

Mulberries turned green when we bade adieu;
I'm not yet back half-red persimmons hang.
You can't match a country wife who does know
When to pestle clothes for her man, bang, bang.

* mulberry: the edible, berry-like fruit of a tree (genus *Morus*) whose leaves are valued for silkworm culture, and the tree itself, first cultivated in the drainage area of the Yellow River in China about five thousand years ago, concurrent with the time when silkworms were raised.
* persimmon: a tree of the ebony family, bearing orange-red or yellow plum-like fruit, very astringent until exposed to frost.

赠　　内

漠漠暗苔新雨地，
微微凉露欲秋天。
莫对月明思往事，
损君颜色减君年。

To My Wife

Dim, dim, the moss aground washed by a rain,
Bit, bit, autumn's coming with chilly dew.
Don't think of the past, looking at the moon,
As fades your charm, subtracting years from you.

* moss: a tiny, delicate green bryophytic plant growing on damp decaying wood, wet ground, humid rocks or trees, producing capsules which open by an operculum and contain spores. Under a poet's writing brush, this tiny, insignificant plant may arouse a poetic feeling or imagination, as was written by Mei Yüan, a poet in the Ching dynasty: "Where the sun does not arrive, /Springtime does on its own thrive. / The moss flowers like rice tiny, / Rush to bloom like the peony."

寄江南兄弟

分散骨肉恋，
趋驰名利牵。
一奔尘埃马，
一泛风波船。
忽忆分手时，
悯默秋风前。
别来朝复夕，
积日成七年。
花落城中地，
春深江上天。
登楼东南望，
鸟灭烟苍然。
相去复几许？
道里近三千。
平地犹难见，
况乃隔山川。

A Letter to My Brothers in the South

Apart, we miss each other dear;
I'm running to gain fame or note!
Running always, my horse astride,
Or blown on by wind in a boat.
Our parting there occurs to me:
Sad, silent in the autumn sough.
As time has gone off and gone by,

The days have made seven years now.
Spring deepens on the river blue;
Flowers in the town fall to the ground.
I go upstairs, southeast I gaze;
In the haze no birds can be found.
How far are we like this apart?
A thousand miles it seems to be.
It's hard to meet e'en on a plain;
Mountains and rivers all fret me!

寄 行 简

郁郁眉多敛，
默默口寡言。
岂是愿如此，
举目谁与欢。
去春尔西征，
从事巴蜀间。
今春我南谪，
抱疾江海壖。
相去六千里，
地绝天邈然。
十书九不达，
何以开忧颜。
渴人多梦饮，
饥人多梦餐。
春来梦何处，
合眼到东川。

To Hsingchien, My Brother

Sad, sad, so knitted are my brows;
Mute, mute, nothing I'd like to say.
Do I want to be so, like this?
All in my sight, who'll share my day?
You went west on the march last spring
To Pa and Shu, their hill and rill.
I'm deposed to the south this spring,

By river and plain, lying ill.
The land rolls far, the sky looks high;
We are apart, three thousand miles.
Nine out of ten letters are lost;
What can turn sadness into smiles?
One who's hungry eats in his dream;
One who's thirsty in his dream drinks;
Now spring's in, what's he dreaming of?
He's arrived at East Shu in blinks.

* Pa: an ancient state referring to an area covering present-day Double Gain (Ch'ungch'ing), the east of Ssuch'uan, the west of Hupei, and north of Kuichow and the northwest of Hunan.
* Shu: a former name for Ssuch'uan, one of the earliest kingdoms in China, founded by Silkworm according to legend. In the Three Kingdoms period, a new Shu was established by Pei Liu, hence one of the three kingdoms in that period.
* East Shu: the east part of today's Ssuchu'an Province.

闻龟儿咏诗

怜渠已解咏诗章,
摇膝支颐学二郎。
莫学二郎吟太苦,
才年四十鬓如霜。

On Hearing Tortoise Chanting a Poem

A verse you can now chant, what a cute boy!
Like me, your knees you sway and chin uphold.
Don't learn from me to suffer too much pain;
I've sideburns frost-white at forty years old.

* Tortoise: Pai's nephew, a little child at that time.

哭崔儿

掌珠一颗儿三岁，
鬓雪千茎父六旬。
岂料汝先为异物，
常忧吾不见成人。
悲肠自断非因剑，
啼眼加昏不是尘。
怀抱又空天默默，
依前重作邓攸身。

Mourning Ts'ui, My Son

Son, you're three years old, a pearl on my palm;
Three score I am, my sideburns crop like snow.
Now you have rushed down to the other world,
And I've ne'er seen you a grown-up, my woe.
It's not the sword that cuts my bowels to bleed;
It's not the dust that blurs my eyes, so dim.
My arms void now, I face the silent sky;
I've lost you, like Righteous Teng, like him.

* Righteous Teng: Yu Teng, a minister in the Chin dynasty. In the havoc of the Revolt of Five Hun Nations, great multitudes fled to the south. During this escape, to relieve the cumber, he tied his own baby to a tree and continued to flee, carrying his nephew on his back. As a result, for the protection of his nephew, he lost his own son.

感　情

中庭晒服玩，
忽见故乡履。
昔赠我者谁，
东邻婵娟子。
因思赠时语，
特用结终始。
永愿如履綦，
双行复双止。
自吾谪江郡，
飘荡三千里。
为感长情人，
提携同到此。
今朝一惆怅，
反覆看未已。
人只履犹双，
何曾得相似。
可嗟复可惜，
锦表绣为里。
况经梅雨来，
色黯花草死。

Love of the Shoes

I find a pair of shoes from home,
As I put my clothing to air;
Who is it that gave them to me?

My east neighbor called Luna Fair.
I think of what she told me then:
Where'er you go, they are for you.
May our friendship go like the shoes;
In two they go, they rest in two.
Now I am banished to Chiangchow,
Away from home, three thousand *li*;
I think back on her full of love,
So glad to have brought them with me;
Today I sigh, the shoes in hand,
Looking at them once and again;
I'm just one, but the shoes are two;
When can we meet so to be twain?
O my long grief and my long sigh:
They're brocade out and silk inside!
The mould rain season has come on;
Their hue's off and their flowers have died.

* mould rain season: alias plum rain season. The warm brought in by monsoons from the Pacific Ocean causes continuous rain in middle and lower reaches of the Long River, Taiwan area, and middle and southern parts of Japan and southern parts of South Korea during June and July, when plums are ripe, hence plum rain.

开元九诗书卷

红笺白纸两三束,
半是君诗半是书。
经年不展缘身病,
今日开看生蠹鱼。

Opening Chen Yüan's Works

Red pads, white sheets, in bundles two or three,
Half of them be your verse, half your scripts be.
I haven't touched them, so ill for a year;
Now I ope them and find bookworms appear.

* Chen Yüan: Chen Yüan (A.D. 779 - A.D. 831), a famous T'ang poet, Pai's closest friend, the two forming a dyad in the history of Chinese Literature.
* bookworms: any various insects destructive to books, especially one of the order *Corrodentia*.

蓝桥驿见元九诗

蓝桥春雪君归日，
秦岭秋风我去时。
每到驿亭先下马，
循墙绕柱觅君诗。

Reading Chen Yüan's Poem at Blue Bridge Post

Homebound, you passed Blue Bridge in spring snow;
Blown south, I watched Ch'in Ridge's autumn hue.
Once at a post, I would dismount my steed
And would find your verse on the wall to read

* Blue Bridge Post: Blue Bridge is on the Blue Stream in Blue Field County under today's Sha'anhsi Province, where was instituted a post.
* steed: a horse; especially a spirited war horse. The use of horses in war can be traced back to the Shang dynasty (1600 B.C.- 1046 B.C.), when a department of horse management was established. A verse from *The Book of Songs* tells of Lord Civil of Watch's industriousness: "In state affairs he leads; / He has three thousand steeds."

寄生衣与微之,因题封上

浅色縠衫轻似雾,
纺花纱袴薄于云。
莫嫌轻薄但知著,
犹恐通州热杀君。

Sending Summer Clothes to Weichih, Written on the Wrap

White is the shirt, as light as misty air;
The cotton trousers are thin like clouds fleet.
Don't think that they are too flimsy to wear;
I fear in Tung you might be killed by heat.

* Weichih: one of Chen Yüan's courtesy names. In A.D. 815, he was appointed to serve as a marshal in Tung, near today's Tachow, Ssuch'uan Province.
* cotton: the soft, white seed hairs filling the seedpods of various shrubby plants of the mallow family, originally native to the tropics, introduced to China in the Western Han dynasty.

舟中读元九诗

把君诗卷灯前读，
诗尽灯残天未明。
眼痛灭灯犹暗坐，
逆风吹浪打船声。

Reading Chen Yüan's Poems on a Boat

I read your book of verses in the light,
It's finished and the light tapers at night.
Eyes sore and light out, I sit alone;
Go-go, my boat by adverse wind is blown.

* Chen Yüan: a famous T'ang poet, Pai's best friend.

初与元九别后忽梦见之及寤而书适至兼寄桐花诗，怅然感怀，因以此寄

永寿寺中语，
新昌坊北分。
归来数行泪，
悲事不悲君。
悠悠蓝田路，
自去无消息。
计君食宿程，
已过商山北。
昨夜云四散，
千里同月色。
晓来梦见君，
应是君相忆。
梦中握君手，
问君意何如。
君言苦相忆，
无人可寄书。
觉来未及说，
叩门声冬冬。
言是商州使，
送君书一封。
枕上忽惊起，
颠倒著衣裳。
开缄见手札，
一纸十三行。
上论迁谪心，
下说离别肠。

心肠都未尽，
不暇叙炎凉。
云作此书夜，
夜宿商州东。
独对孤灯坐，
阳城山馆中。
夜深作书毕，
山月向西斜。
月下何所有，
一树紫桐花。
桐花半落时，
复道正相思。
殷勤书背后，
兼寄桐花诗。
桐花诗八韵，
思绪一何深。
以我今朝意，
忆君此夜心。
一章三遍读，
一句十回吟。
珍重八十字，
字字化为金。

After Parting from Chen Yüan, I Dreamed of Him; when I Awoke, His Letter and Verse of Chinese Scholar Tree Flower Arrived. Therefore, So Perturbed, I Wrote This.

In Long Life Temple there we talked

And we parted in New Boom Lane.
Now back, I'd a few strings of tears;
It's things, not you that have caused pain.
The Blue Field road rolls and rolls on;
No news of yours has arrived e'er.
I reckon by how fast you go
You must have passed Mt. Shang north there.
Last night clouds dispersed all around;
The moonlight spread a thousand *li*.
Towards the dawn, I dreamed of you;
You must have also thought of me.
In the dream I took your hand
And asked how you were getting on.
You said that you missed me so much;
But to send letters there was none.
I woke — nothing I said but heard
Knocks on the door and knocks anew.
A messenger from Shang he was
Who brought me a letter from you.
I rose suddenly and in haste
Put on my vesture inside out.
I opened your letter right now
A sheet of thirteen lines throughout.
You talked about your demotion
And then about your parting keen.
You talked and talked on without end,
But not enough of how you'd been.
At night this letter you composed;
East of Shang you slept for the night.
In the hill hostel at Sun Town,
You sat alone in the lamp light.

You finished the letter at night,
When the moon would sink in the west.
What was there under the pale moon?
A phoenix tree in mauve flowers dressed.
The phoenix tree flowers had half gone,
And I thought of you just that hour.
On the back of the letter there
You wrote the verse *Phoenix Tree Flower*.
Phoenix Tree Flower, in sixteen lines,
Expresses your emotion smart.
This morning here I feel so touched
With your love that night, your keen heart.
Your verse I read once and again
Chanting ten time for every line.
So precious are the eighty words,
Each turning into gold to shine.

* In A.D. 809, Chen Yüan was banished to fill a small post at River Ridge that is today's Chingchow, Hupei Province.
* New Boom: what is probably modern New Boom (Hsinch'ang) in Chechiang Province, where Pai was once a prefect.
* Blue Field: Blue Field County under today's Hsi-an, Sha'anhsi Province, famous for jade mined there, called Blue Field Jade.
* Mt. Shang: southeast of Shanglo in modern Sha'anhsi Province, famous for the four Wordist hermits, Ping T'ang, Kuang Ts'ui, Shih Wu and Shu Chou, who were invited as Highsire of Han's thinktank in the early years of Han.
* Sun Town: Sun Town County, located at the southeast end of today's Shanhsi Province.
* Phoenix Tree: Chinese parasol tree, so named because phoenixes perch on Chinese parasol trees.

商山路驿桐树,昔与微之前后题名处

与君前后多迁谪,
五度经过此路隅。
笑问中庭老桐树,
这回归去免来无?

Halting at a Phoenix Tree on the Way by Mt. Shang; Chen Yüan and I Both Left Our Inscriptions Here

We both have been banished often till now;
Five times we've passed this crotch no matter how.
While laughing, I ask the old phoenix tree:
Whether this could be the last one for me.

* Chen Yüan: Chen Yüan (A.D. 779 – A.D. 831), a famous T'ang poet, Pai's closest friend, the two forming a dyad in the history of Chinese Literature.
* Phoenix Tree: Chinese parasol tree, so named because phoenixes perch on Chinese parasol trees.

梦与李七、庾三十三同访元九

夜梦归长安,
见我故亲友。
损之在我左,
顺之在我右。
云是二月天,
春风出携手。
同过靖安里,
下马寻元九。
元九正独坐,
见我笑开口。
还指西院花,
仍开北亭酒。
如言各有故,
似惜欢难久。
神合俄顷间,
神离欠伸后。
觉来疑在侧,
求索无所有。
残灯影闪墙,
斜月光穿牖。
天明西北望,
万里君知否。
老去无见期,
踟蹰搔白首。

My Dream of Visiting Chen Yüan with Li Seven and Yü Thirty-Three

Last night I dreamed of Long Peace, where
I met with my friends with delight.
Sun Chih was there on my left hand
And Shun Chih was here on my right.
They said it was just early spring,
Why not go for fun in spring air.
We galloped through Peaceful Lane and,
Dismounting, asked about Chen, where?
There, Chen Nine, was sitting alone;
At sight of me, he smiled to shine.
Pointing at the flowers in West Court,
He'd open North Pavilion wine.
He seemed to say we live apart,
No much chance for a happy day.
So briefly we've enjoyed our glee;
Once we part, the glee goes away.
I woke, as if he were beside;
I looked, he was nowhere in sight.
The lamp did flicker to the wall;
The moon thru the window sent light.
The day breaking, northwest I gazed;
Do you know this, far, far away?
When can we meet now we are old?
In sadness, I scratch my hair gray.

---

* Long Peace: Ch'ang'an if transliterated, the metropolis of gold, the capital of the

T'ang, the largest city in the world then, with a population of one million. As the starting point of the Silk Road and the birthplace of Chinese civilization, it has been a capital for thirteen dynasties, enjoying the privilege of the Museum of Chinese History, and it is now the capital of Sha'anhsi Province.

* Sun Chih: Ts'ungmin Li, dubbed Sun Chih.
* Shun Chih: Chinghsiu Yü, Yü Thirty-three, dubbed Shun Chih.
* Peaceful Lane: a lane in Long Peace.

赠梦得

年颜老少与君同，
眼未全昏耳未聋。
放醉卧为春日伴，
趁欢行入少年丛。
寻花借马烦川守，
弄水偷船恼令公。
闻道洛城人尽怪，
呼为刘白二狂翁。

To Yühsi Liu

You and me, we were born in the same year,
Ears not yet deaf, eyes not having lost sight.
Now spring's coming on, let's go and lie drunk
And join the crowd of youngsters with delight.
To borrow steeds, we fret the magistrate;
And stealing a boat, we make the boatman sad.
It seems people in Loshine all blame us,
Shouting: Liu and Pai, you two old men mad!

* Yühsi Liu: Yühsi Liu (A.D. 772 - A.D. 842), a famous poet and philosopher, Pai's old friend.
* Loshine: Loyang if transliterated, one of the four ancient capitals in China, along with Long Peace (Hsi'an), Gold Hill (Nanking) and Peking, and it was the second largest city and the eastern capital of the T'ang dynasty, with a population of 800,000. It was first built from 1735 B.C. to 1540 B.C. in the Hsia dynasty as its political center, and in 1046 B.C. Prince of Chough built two cities here in order to control Chough's east

territory. In 770 B.C. King Peace of Chough moved to this place when Warmer (Haoching), Chough's capital, was captured by Hounds (Ch'üanjung), hence the Eastern Chough dynasty. Since its founding, Loshine has been a capital for thirteen dynasties.

久不见韩侍郎,戏题四韵以寄之

近来韩阁老,
疏我我心知。
户大嫌甜酒,
才高笑小诗。
静吟乘月夜,
闲醉旷花时。
还有愁同处,
春风满鬓丝。

I Haven't Seen Vice Premier for Long, So I Send Him Four Couplets for Fun

Recently, dear Han, o my lord,
I know that you leave me ignored.
My wine's crude to you, dignified,
And my small verse you may deride.
Let's trill before the moon is sunk;
And mid the sea of flowers lie drunk.
If worried, we have the same care,
Let the spring wind fill in our hair.

* dear Han: Yü Han (A.D. 768 – A.D. 824), from Rivershine in today's Honan Province, a litterateur, thinker, philosopher and politician in the T'ang dynasty.

以 镜 赠 别

人言似明月，
我道胜明月。
明月非不明，
一年十二缺。
岂如玉匣里，
如水常澄澈。
月破天暗时，
圆明独不歇。
我惭貌丑老，
绕鬓斑斑雪。
不如赠少年，
回照青丝发。
因君千里去，
持此将为别。

A Mirror as a Parting Present

All say it is bright like the moon;
I think it better than the moon.
It's not the moon's not bright and clear;
It wanes for twelve times in a year.
The mirror in a box of jade
Is like water so limpid made.
When the moon is sunk and it's dim;
It's still round and bright to the brim.
Now I'm so old, an ugly sight,

With drooping sideburns like snow white.
I'd better give this glass to you,
A youth with black hair shining new.
As you're going far, far away,
Take this as a gift with you, pray.

* the moon: the celestial body that revolves around the earth from west to east as a satellite, which appears at night and gives off shining silvery light, an image of purity and solitude in Chinese culture.
* glass: a mirror or a metaphor for a mirror. A kind of glass may have been introduced into China from Egypt in the T'ang dynasty.

访陶公旧宅

垢尘不污玉，
灵凤不啄膻。
呜呼陶靖节，
生彼晋宋间。
心实有所守，
口终不能言。
永惟孤竹子，
拂衣首阳山。
夷齐各一身，
穷饿未为难。
先生有五男，
与之同饥寒。
肠中食不充，
身上衣不完。
连征竟不起，
斯可谓真贤。
我生君之后，
相去五百年。
每读五柳传，
目想心拳拳。
昔常咏遗风，
著为十六篇。
今来访故宅，
森若君在前。
不慕樽有酒，
不慕琴无弦。
慕君遗容利，

老死此丘园。
柴桑古村落，
栗里旧山川。
不见篱下菊，
但馀墟中烟。
子孙虽无闻，
族氏犹未迁。
每逢姓陶人，
使我心依然。

A Visit to Poolbright T'ao's Old House

Dust or dirt does not soil a jade;
A phoenix eats not meat decayed.
O Poolbright T'ao, a man so sage
Lived between Chin and Sung, that age.
In his heart he had faith so stout,
Which he'd never ever speak out.
He did learn from the righteous men,
Who withdrew to Mt. Firstshine then.
Bowone and Straightthree did abide
In want and hunger till they died.
In all Mister T'ao had five sons,
Who all lived in need, all great ones.
No food in their bowels so hard pressed,
And their bodies not wholly dressed.
Frequently called, they did not rise,
Really virtuous, and truly wise.
I was born after him, far way;
It's five hundred years to a day.

With his *Five Willows* I'm entranced,
And my spirit's highly enhanced.
I'd sing highly of what has been
And have written verses sixteen.
I visit his old house today,
As if he did still in here stay.
I don't admire his wine-filled pot;
His stringless lute I admire not.
I do admire his looks profound,
His body buried neath the mound.
Behold the old Mulberry Town,
With chestnut trees uphill and down.
His hedge chrysanthemums not there
But smoke curling up in the air.
Though his descendants are unknown,
The clan's not moved, raised on their own.
Whenever one named T'ao I see,
So much perturbed my heart will be.

* Poolbright T'ao: Yüanming T'ao (A.D. 352 – A.D. 427) if transliterated, a complex figure and a poet of complex poems — a verse writer, poet, and litterateur in the Chin dynasty, and the founder of Chinese idyllism, who was once the magistrate of P'engtse.
* phoenix: a legendary bird of great beauty, unique of its kind, which was supposed to live five or six hundred years before consuming itself by fire, rising again from its ashes to live through another cycle, a symbol of immortality. In Chinese mythology, the phoenix only perches on phoenix trees, i.e. firmiana, only eats firmiana fruit, and only drinks sweet spring water, and this mythic bird appears only in times of peace and a sagacious rule.
* Chin and Sung: two kingdoms established during the Southern Dynasties period.
* Firstshine: Mt. Firstshine, located in today's Weiyüan County. It is the highest of all mountains there, so it is the first to receive sunshine, hence the name, and it is famous because two princes from the State of Lonebamboo called Bowone (Po-ee if transliterated) and Straightthree (Shuch'i if transliterated) died of starvation here for

their rectitude.
* *Five Willows*: referring to Poolbright T'ao's *The Biography of Mt. Five Willows*, also an allusion to Mr. Five Willows, alias Ch'ien T'ao (A.D. 352 – A.D. 427) himself, who planted five willows before his doorway when he lived in reclusion.
* chestnut tree: any of the genus (*Castanea*) of trees of the beech family, growing in a prickly bur, bearing smooth shelled, sweet, edible nuts.
* chrysanthemum: any of a genus of perennials of the composite family, some cultivated varieties of which have large heads of showy flowers of various colors, a symbol of elegance and integrity in Chinese culture, one of the four most important floral images in Chinese literature, which are wintersweet, orchid, bamboo, and chrysanthemum.

江南遇天宝乐叟

白头老叟泣且言,
禄山未乱入梨园。
能弹琵琶和法曲,
多在华清随至尊。
是时天下太平久,
年年十月坐朝元。
千官起居环珮合,
万国会同车马奔。
金钿照耀石瓮寺,
兰麝熏煮温汤源。
贵妃宛转侍君侧,
体弱不胜珠翠繁。
冬雪飘飖锦袍暖,
春风荡漾霓裳翻。
欢娱未足燕寇至,
弓劲马肥胡语喧。
豳土人迁避夷狄,
鼎湖龙去哭轩辕。
从此漂沦落南土,
万人死尽一身存。
秋风江上浪无限,
暮雨舟中酒一樽。
涸鱼久失风波势,
枯草曾沾雨露恩。
我自秦来君莫问,
骊山渭水如荒村。
新丰树老笼明月,

长生殿暗锁春云。
红叶纷纷盖欹瓦,
绿苔重重封坏垣。
唯有中官作宫使,
每年寒食一开门。

Coming Across an Old Musician in the South in the Heaven-Blessed Reign

I joined Pear Garden before Lushan's Sway,
Said the gray-haired old man as he did cry.
I could play the pipa and know new scores,
Attending at Flora Pool the Most High.
Then it had been a peaceful time for long;
Dawn Hall would be live the tenth moon each year.
Officials by the thousand clinked and clanged;
Embassies swarmed with steeds and carts and cheer.
Ladies' jewels shone at the temple nearby;
Orchids and musk perfumed the hot spring there.
Jade Ring warbled by His Majesty's side,
So lithe and slender her pearls swayed to glare.
Thru snow spring air sent warmth to damask gowns;
Her plumage dress danced in the tide of spring.
While they played high, from north enemies swept,
Fat steeds, Hun dins, bows bent with a tense string.
The emperor was forced to flee the foes,
And as His cart was gone, all people cried.
Now I drift like down in the southern land,
A lonely soul, as ten thousand have died.
On the river autumn wind throws up waves,

In dust rain, I face a cup of wine aboard.
The dried fish has lost wind and tide for long;
The dried grass has no more dew from the Lord.
Don't ask me, who has come here from the west,
Where Mt. Black Steed and the Wei are all dried.
In Newrich, old trees are veiled by the moon;
Long Life Hall is by black clouds occupied.
Broken tiles on the roofs strewn with red leaves;
Fallen walls humid with moss, with moss mere.
The eunuchs left there but performs some rites,
Oping gates at Cold Food Day once a year.

* Heaven-Blessed: one of the reign titles of Empire Deepsire, fifteen years from A.D. 742 to A.D. 756.
* Pear Garden: an operatic school established by Emperor Deepsire, where actors and actresses were trained, and the prototype of the modern Chinese drama was developed.
* Lushan: Lushan An(A.D. 703 – A.D. 757), of the Kitan race, who distinguished himself in fighting against his own tribes, won the favor of Jade Ring and the confidence of Emperor Deepsire. His promotion being rapid, he was ennobled as a count, and made the governor of the border provinces of the north, where he held under command the best armies of the empire and nursed an inordinate ambition to own the empire. At one stage in their relationship, Jade Ring (Imperial Concubine Yang) made the rebel Lushan An her adopted son.
* Flora Pool: a resort at Flora Palace in one of the four most famous royal parks in China, built in the T'ang dynasty.
* the Most High: referring to Emperor Deepsire.
* Dawn Hall: one of halls in Flora Palace.
* orchid: any of a widely distributed family of terrestrial or epiphytic monocotyledonous plants having thickened bulbous roots and often very showy distinctive flowers, one of the four most important floral images in Chinese literature, which are wintersweet, orchid, bamboo, and chrysanthemum.
* musk: a soft, reddish-brown powdery secretion of a penetrating odor, obtained from the preputial follicles of the male musk deer, used by perfumers and in medicine.
* Jade Ring: Lady Yang (A.D. 719 – A.D. 756), Deepsire the Emperor's Imperial

Consort, a talented musician, one of the four beauties in Chinese history, the loveliest of the three thousand palace ladies of T'ang, ever accompanying the emperor's palanquin, singing and dancing to him.

* Mt. Black Steed: the mountain south of Lintung, an important offset of Mt. Ch'in Ridge, 1,302 meters above sea level, the location of the royal palace of Ch'in and tomb of Emperor First.
* the Wei: the Wei River: the largest branch of the Yellow River, originating from today's Mt. Birdmouse in Kansu Province, flowing through Precious Rooster, Allshine, Long Peace, and meeting the Yellow River at T'ung Pass.
* Newrich: a county, built by Pang Liu in imitation of his hometown Rich County, in today's Lintung County, Sha'anhsi Province, famous for its wine, the best wine in the T'ang dynasty.
* Cold Food Day: one or two days before Pure Brightness Day, the festival in memory of Chiht'ui of Chieh (? - 636 B.C.) observed without cooking for a day. In the Spring and Autumn period, Double Ear, a prince of Chin, escaped from the disaster in his state with his follower Chiht'ui. In great deprivation, Double Ear almost starved to death, and Chiht'ui fed him with flesh cut off his thigh. When Double Ear was crowned as Lord Civil of Chin, Chiht'ui retreated to Mt. Silk Floss with his mother when feeling neglected. To have him out, Lord Civil set the mountain on fire, but Chiht'ui did not give in and was burned with his mother, hugging a tree.

东楼招客夜饮

莫辞数数醉东楼，
除醉无因破得愁。
唯有绿樽红烛下，
暂时不似在忠州。

Inviting Guests to a Drink on East Tower

Don't ask how oft I'm drunk on the east tower;
If not drunk, how could I dispel my woe?
But candle and wine give me a good hour,
So that I'd forget my post in Chungchow.

* Chungchow: what is now Chunghsien County in today's Ch'ungch'ing.

故　　衫

暗淡绯衫称老身，
半披半曳出朱门。
袖中吴郡新诗本，
襟上杭州旧酒痕。
残色过梅看向尽，
故香因洗嗅犹存。
曾经烂熳三年著，
欲弃空箱似少恩。

My Old Gown

The dark scarlet gown fits me well, so great;
It half draping, I go out of Red Gate.
The sleeve hides a new book of Wu Town verse;
The front sees wine stains from Hangchow disperse.
The sign of plums has faded, almost gone;
The fragrance, although washed off, lingers on.
It keeps alive the three years of my best;
How heartless if it's cast to the void chest!

* Red Gate: a metonymy for an official office.
* Wu Town: referring to Soochow, where Pai was its prefect for seventeen months.
* Hangchow: the capital of today's Chechiang Province, where Pai was its prefect for three years.
* plum: a kind of plant or the edible purple drupaceous fruit of the plant which is any one of various trees of the genus *Prunus*, cultivated in temperate zones.

读李杜诗集因题卷后

翰林江左日，
员外剑南时。
不得高官职，
仍逢苦乱离。
暮年逋客恨，
浮世谪仙悲。
吟咏流千古，
声名动四夷。
文场供秀句，
乐府待新词。
天意君须会，
人间要好诗。

Reading Li and Tu's Collection of Poems, Hence My Inscription on the Back Cover

To south Brushwood Li was exiled;
And Works Tu fled south to Sword Pass.
No important posts did they hold,
Suffering chaos and pains, alas.
In his last years Tu complained much;
Drifting here and there, Li much sighed.
Their odes and hymns will last for e'er;
And their renown will spread worldwide.
All Muses come out with good works;
Yüehfu expects new style to start.

God's will we all should understand:
The human world needs the best art.

* Brushwood Li: referring to Pai Li (A.D. 701 - A.D. 762), who once had a sinecure in Brushwood Academy. Pai Li, Venus by courtesy name and Green Lotus and Exiled Immortal by literary names, an excellent romantic poet in the T'ang dynasty, has been praised as "God of Poetry". According to *New Book of T'ang*, Li descended from Emperor Hsuansheng (i.e. Li Hao, Lord Martial Glare of Liang), and had the same ancestry with the royal family, the Li House in the T'ang dynasty. He was hearty, generous, and keen on drinking, composing poems and making friends.
* Works Tu: referring to Fu Tu (A.D. 712 - A.D. 770), who once held a sinecure in the Department of Works. Fu Tu, Tsumei by courtesy name and Shaolin's Old & Alone Master of None by literary name, born in Sowshine, Hubei Province. Later he moved to Kunghsien County, Honan Province.
* Sword Pass: a strategic pass with a plank road built along cliffs by Bright Chuke in the Three Kingdoms period, in present-day Ssuch'uan Province. In this poem it is a metonymy for Ssuch'uan.
* Muses: a metaphor for great poets. They are nine goddesses who preside over literature and the arts and sciences in Greek Mythology.
* Yüehfu: Conservatoire, which might be otherwise called Music Hall or Music Bureau. It was an ancient official organization for the management of music and poetry, specifically responsible for the collection, adaptation, composition, and performance of musical and poetic works, initially instituted in Ch'in and formally established in 112 B.C., the age of Emperor Martial of Han.

听 夜 筝 有 感

江州去日听筝夜，
白发新生不愿闻。
如今格是头成雪，
弹到天明亦任君。

Perturbed at the Cheng at Night

In Bankshine at night, I oft heard the cheng;
I would not listen, hair mine newly gray.
Now my head has suddenly become snow;
Till daybreak, the cheng you can freely play.

* cheng: a Chinese musical instrument like the zither with twenty one or twenty five strings, commonly played by men of letters during the T'ang dynasty.
* Bankshine: formally called Riverton, most part of today's Chianghsi Province. It was one of the prefectures of T'ang.

放言五首(选三)
Bold Words, Five Poems (Three out of Five)

其 一

朝真暮伪何人辨,
古往今来底事无?
但爱臧生能诈圣,
可知宁子解伴愚?
草萤有耀终非火,
荷露虽团岂是珠?
不取燔柴兼照乘,
可怜光彩亦何殊!

No. 1

It's false at dusk and true at dawn, who can tell?
No such things before or now? What the hell?
All hypocrites feign to be saints by rule;
Who knows a clever man may seem a fool?
Fireflies are not fire though they brightly glow;
Grass dews are not pearls though they luster show.
Fuels aren't used to both cook and light a car;
They have the same light but different they are!

* firefly: any of a family (*Lampyridae*) of winged beetles, active at night, whose abdomens usually glow with a luminescent light.
* pearl: a lustrous, calcareous concretion deposited in layers around a central nucleus in the shells of various mollusks, and largely used as a gem or regarded as a treasure or given as a gift to represent love and friendship.

其 二

世途倚伏都无定，
尘网牵缠卒未休。
祸福回还车转毂，
荣枯反覆手藏钩。
龟灵未免刳肠患，
马失应无折足忧。
不信君看弈棋者，
输赢须待局终头。

No. 2

The world is uncertain, to rise or fall;
A net it is, entangled and entwined.
Bliss or bane, a whirligig, turns for all;
Well or ill, a hook's hid in hand behind.
A tortoise is cut open to foretell;
If a horse slips, don't worry, you need not.
Look at the chess, how it is played, how well;
Only the end of the game shows the lot.

* tortoise: a turtle, especially one that lives on land, as any of a worldwide family.
* horse: a large solid-hoofed quadruped (*Equus caballus*) with coarse mane and tail, of various strains — Ferghana, Mongolian, Kazaks, Hequ, Karasahr and so on and of various colors — black, white, yellow, brown, dappled and so on, commonly in the domesticated state, employed as a beast of draught and burden and especially for riding upon. It is one of the earliest domesticated animals in Chinese culture, widely used in wars and owned as property in powerful families.

其 四

谁家第宅成还破，
何处亲宾哭复歌。
昨日屋头堪炙手，
今朝门外好张罗。
北邙未省留闲地，
东海何曾有定波。
莫笑贱贫夸富贵，
共成枯骨两如何。

No. 4

Whose mansions are built and are soon to fall?
Whose relatives and friends sing and then squall?
Once his house swarmed with so many a head;
Now on the doorway traps and snares are spread.
No spare fields are left on the Northern Hill;
Can East Sea have breakers or ripples still?
Do not laugh at those low or praise those high;
Both would be rotten bones after they die.

* the Northern Hill: the hill north of Loshine, where one can see many tombs of the lords and peers of the Eastern Han dynasty and the Northern Way dynasty.
* East Sea: what is known as East China Sea today, with an area of 770 thousand square kilometers.

登商山最高顶

高高此山顶，
四望唯烟云。
下有一条路，
通达楚与秦。
或名诱其心，
或利牵其身。
乘者及负者，
来去何云云。
我亦斯人徒，
未能出嚣尘。
七年三往复，
何得笑他人。

Climbing to the Apex of Mt. Shang

High, high the apex of Mt. Shang,
You see all mist and smoke around.
There extends a road down below,
And for Ch'u and Ch'in it is bound.
Lo, those who go for some renown;
Lo, those who to riches have bowed.
Those riders and those carriers there
Make haste, single or in a crowd.
I am one of them I should say,
Who to all world affairs is tied.
I've shuttled thrice in seven years;

How could I other men deride?

* Mt. Shang: also known as the South Hills, famous for the four Wordist hermits, Ping T'ang, Kuang Ts'ui, Shih Wu and Shu Chou, who were invited as Highsire of Han's think tank in the early years of Han.
* Ch'u: the State of Ch'u, a large vassal state under Chough, one of the powers in the Warring States period, conquered and annexed by Ch'in in 223 B.C.
* Ch'in: the Ch'in State or the State of Ch'in (905 B.C. – 206 B.C.), one of the most powerful vassal states in the Chough dynasty, which developed into the first unified regime of China, i.e., the Ch'in Empire.

秋　蝶

秋花紫蒙蒙，
秋蝶黄茸茸。
花低蝶新小，
飞戏丛西东。
日暮凉风来，
纷纷花落丛。
夜深白露冷，
蝶已死丛中。
朝生夕俱死，
气类各相从。
不见千年鹤，
多栖百丈松。

An Autumn Butterfly

The autumn flowers are purple hued,
The butterfly in yellow dressed.
The flowers low, the butterfly small,
The latter seeks fun east and west.
At dusk a cold wind blows along;
Some flowers are stirred to fall aground.
Night deep, the white frost feels so cold,
The butterfly's died, as is found.
At down he's born, at night you die;
All will arise and all will fall.
Have you e'er seen an age-old crane

Perched on a pine score score feet tall?

* butterfly: any of various families of lepidopteran insects active in the day-time, having a sucking mouthpart, slender body, ropelike, knobbed antennae, and four broad, usually brightly colored, membraneous wings.
* crane: one of a family of large, long-necked, long-legged, heronlike birds allied to the rails, a symbol of longevity and integrity in Chinese culture, only second to the phoenix in cultural importance.
* pine: any of a genus (*Pinus*) of evergreen trees of the pine family, a cone-bearing tree having bundles of two to five needle-shaped leaves growing in clusters, one of the most important images in Chinese literature, a symbol of rectitude, longevity and so on.

别草堂三绝句
Farewell to Thatched Cottage, Three Quatrains

其 一

正听山鸟向阳眠，
黄纸除书落枕前。
为感君恩须暂起，
炉峰不拟住多年。

No. 1

In sunlit bed I, listen to hill birds;
The rescript comes with the Lord's words.
I must rise now to thank His grace;
I won't live long on Mt. Lodge, this good place.

* Thatched Cottage: Chü-e Pai owned a thatched cottage by Mt. Censer on Mt. Lodge. The rescript from Long Peace directed him to go to Chungchow.
* Mt. Lodge: a famous mountain with historic, cultural and religious attractions, an especially sacred place to Wordists, about 5,000 feet high, in present-day Chianghsi Province.

其 二

久眠褐被为居士，
忽挂绯袍作使君。
身出草堂心不出，
庐山未要勒移文。

No. 2

I've been a hermit in plain clothes for long;
Now I'm a prefect wearing a red gown.
I'm out of my thatched shack, but my heart not;
Mt. Lodge is where I'd like to settle down.

* thatched shack: a metonymy for hermitage in traditional Chinese culture, like hills and seas, nature, moors and so on.
* Mt. Lodge: a famous mountain, about 5,000 feet high, with historic, cultural and religious attractions, abundant with caves, ravines, grotesque rocks and cataracts, an especially sacred place to Wordists, located in present-day Chianghsi Province.

其 三

三间茅舍向山开,
一带山泉绕舍回。
山色泉声莫惆怅,
三年官满却归来。

No. 3

Three rooms of thatch are opened to the hill;
A belt of fountain gurgles around my shack.
Don't release a sigh like the gurgling spring,
In three years, my term o'er, I will come back.

* Three rooms of thatch are opened to the hill: Pai had a cottage built at Mt. Lodge and wrote quite a few poems on it.

新乐府五十首（选二十二）
New Conservertoire, Fifty Poems (Twenty-two out of Fifty)

海漫漫

海漫漫，
直下无底旁无边；
云涛烟浪最深处，
人传中有三神山。
山上多生不死药，
服之羽化为天仙。
秦皇汉武信此语，
方士年年采药去。
蓬莱今古但闻名，
烟水茫茫无觅处。
海漫漫，风浩浩，
眼穿不见蓬莱岛。
不见蓬莱不敢归，
童男丱女舟中老。
徐福文成多诳诞，
上元太一虚祈祷。
君看骊山顶上茂陵头，
毕竟悲风吹蔓草！
何况玄元圣祖五千言，
不言药，不言仙，
不言白日升青天。

The Surging Vast Sea

The surging vast sea,
A bottom there is not, bounds there can't be.
In the depth of the waves and clouds so spread,
There are three fairy mountains, as is said.
In the mountains there is made a cure-all;
One taken, one's in Heaven, ne'er to fall.
When lords like Emperor First did this hear,
Wordists were sent for it year after year.
The P'englai Isles have been known since the past;
But they're not to be found, the sea so vast.
The surging sea vast, where wind does blow fast;
The P'englai Isles are nowhere, eyes surpassed.
Not seeing the Isles, they dared not return
Boys, girls in boats got old, their hearts did burn.
Bliss Hsu and Accomplished Wen, what a gain!
To Lady Up and Void they prayed in vain.
Lo and behold, Mt. Black Steed and the Lush Ridge, alas,
Where a sad wind blows across rampant grass.
Haven't you heard the Dark Emperor's *Five Thousand Words* read?
Mentioning no drugs, nor fays, and nor days
You will be risen to the sky instead.

---

* Emperor First: Emperor First (259 B.C.- 210 B.C.), the founding emperor of Ch'in who wiped out all the other states and established the first unified empire in China. He was universally acknowledged as a great politician, strategist, reformer, and an iron hand tyrant, who laid the political layout of China after the Ch'in dynasty till now.
* Wordist: one who believes in or professes belief of Wordism, the doctrines declared by Laocius (571 B.C.- 471 B.C.). In the T'ang dynasty, while Confucianism remained the guiding principle of state and social morality, Wordism had gathered an incrustation of

mythology and superstition and became popular with both the court and the commoners. Laocius, the founder, was claimed by the reigning dynasty as its remote progenitor and was honored with an imperial title, Emperor Dark One.

* P'englai Isles: also known as Fair Isles, Mt. Fairyland or Fairyland, the three fairy isles held up by giant turtles in East Sea, a dwelling place of immortals and exalted spirits, which has been regarded as today's P'englai in Shantung Province.
* Bliss Hsu: a Wordist (Taoist as is generally called) and alchemist in Ch'in, who tried to find elixir or panacea for the emperor and never returned from Japan on his second trip overseas.
* Wen: referring to Po Wen, a Wordist in the Spring and Autumn period.
* Lady Up: a fairy in Chinese mythology, the youngest daughter of Queen Mother.
* Void: the state of nature. According to *The Word and the World*, "The Word is void." "Void, it's used without end; moved, the more it will send."
* Mt. Black Steed: Sha'anxi Province, is the site of tomb of Emperor First of the Ch'in Dynasty.
* the Lush Ridge: Sha'anxi Province, the site of the tomb of Emperor Martial of Han.
* the Dark Emperor: Emperor Dark One, Laocius, the founder of Wordism, was claimed by the reigning dynasty as its remote progenitor and was honored with an imperial title, Emperor Dark One.
* *Five Thousand Words*: alias *The Word and the World* — the foundational classic of Wordism, written by Laocius (471 B.C.- 571 B.C.), a great philosopher in the Spring and Autumn period. It is the single book that Laocius wrote all his wisdom into.

上阳白发人

上阳人，
红颜暗老白发新。
绿衣监使守宫门，
一闭上阳多少春！
玄宗末岁初选入，
入时十六今六十。
同时采择百馀人，
零落年深残此身。
忆昔吾悲别亲族，
扶入车中不教哭。
皆云入内便承恩，
脸似芙蓉胸似玉。
未容君王得见面，
已被杨妃遥侧目。
妒令潜配上阳宫，
一生遂向空房宿。
宿空房，秋夜长，
夜长无寐天不明。
耿耿残灯背壁影，
萧萧暗雨打窗声。
春日迟，
日迟独坐天难暮。
宫莺百啭愁厌闻，
梁燕双栖老休妒。
莺归燕去长悄然，
春佳秋来不记年。
唯向深宫望明月，
东西四五百回圆。

今日宫中年最老，
大家遥赐尚书号。
小头鞵履窄衣裳，
青黛点眉眉细长。
外人不见见应笑，
天宝末年时世妆。
上阳人，
苦最多。
少亦苦，
老亦苦，
少苦老苦两如何！
君不见昔时吕向《美人赋》，
又不见今日上阳白发歌！

The White-Haired Uppershine Belle

The Uppershine belle,
Her hair's white and her cheeks fade, one can tell.
The palace gate's kept by eunuchs in green.
How many years so immured has she been!
First chosen at the end of Deepsire's reign,
She was sixteen and now sixty to gain.
A hundred beauties were chosen that day,
Now having withered, she's falling to decay.
Then sadly she bade her dear ones good-bye,
When helped to mount, she was told not to cry.
All said once in the harem she'd be blessed,
Her face like a lotus bud, stroked her chest.
But His Majesty has ne'er e'er come by,
Jade Ring casting on her a wary eye.
Being kept in Uppershine but to sigh,

She keeps her vacant room while days go by.
Her vacant room, long her night gloom,
Night gloom sees her sleepless and her soul loom.
Dim, dim, the lamp throws her groan to the wall;
Sough, sough, the dark window hears raindrops fall.
Spring days drag along;
Dragging along, there drags her lonely song.
She's so tired to hear the orioles sing,
The pair of old swallows perched won't her sting.
Orioles come, swallows go, without cheer
Springtime passing, autumn gone, what's the year?
She views the moon above once and again;
Hundreds of times it has changed, wax and wane.
She's been the oldest belle of all today;
Nicknamed Secretary of State with hair gray.
In narrow-headed shoes and thinning gown,
Brows painted with indigo long, long drawn.
At her olden dress outsiders would jest,
Once the fad in the reign of Heaven-Blessed.
The Uppershine belle
Has suffered the hell.
When young, she had pain;
Now old, she has pain.
Young pain, old pain, whatever could she gain?
Don't you espy Hsiang Lü's *Ode to the Belle* in days gone by?
Or you may hear in today's harem *To White Hair You Sigh*.

* Uppershine: a royal palace built in Loshine.
* eunuch: a castrated man in charge of an Oriental harem or employed as a chamberlain or high officer by an Oriental potentate.
* Deepsire: referring to Hsuan Tsung the emperor (A.D. 685 – A.D. 762), the ninth

emperor of the T'ang dynasty. When a prince, he was regarded as wise and valiant, a sportsman accomplished in all knightly exercises and a master of all elegant arts. He established Pear Garden, an operatic school, where actors and actresses were trained, and the prototype of the modern Chinese drama was developed. Under his enthusiastic patronage, arts and letters flourished. Indeed, his reign is often considered the pinnacle of Chinese cultural achievement.

* Jade Ring: Lady Yang (A.D. 719 - A.D. 756), Emperor Deepsire's Imperial Consort, a talented dancer and musician, one of the four beauties in Chinese history, the loveliest of the three thousand palace ladies of T'ang, ever accompanying the emperor's palanquin, singing and dancing to him.
* oriole: golden oriole, one of the family of passerine birds, which looks bright yellow with contrasting black wings and sings beautiful songs.
* swallow: a passerine bird, with short broad, depressed bill, long pointed wings, and forked tail, noted for fleeting flight and migratory habits. In Chinese culture, swallows are welcome to live with a family with their nests on a beam of a sitting room.
* indigo: a blue dye obtained from certain plants, especially a plant native to India, or made synthetically, usually from aniline.
* Heaven - Blessed: one of the reign titles of Empire Deepsire, fifteen years from A.D. 742 to A.D. 756.
* Hsiang Lü: Hsiang Lü (? - A.D. 742), a minister, scholar and calligrapher in the T'ang dynasty.
* *Ode to the Belle*: a euf authored by Hsiang Lü to remonstrate against the beauty pageant and narrates his political values.
* *To White Hair You Sigh*: an imaginary song to fit in with the setting to respond to the song mentioned above.

胡旋女

胡旋女，胡旋女。
心应弦，手应鼓。
弦鼓一声双袖举。
回雪飘飖转蓬舞。
左旋右转不知疲，
千匝万周无已时。
人间物类无可比，
奔车轮缓旋风迟。
曲终再拜谢天子，
天子为之微启齿。
胡旋女，出康居，
徒劳东来万里馀。
中原自有胡旋者，
斗妙争能尔不如。
天宝季年时欲变，
臣妾人人学圆转。
中有太真外禄山，
二人最道能胡旋。
梨花园中册作妃，
金鸡障下养为儿。
禄山胡旋迷君眼，
兵过黄河疑未反。
贵妃胡旋惑君心，
死弃马嵬念更深。
从兹地轴天维转，
五十年来制不禁。
胡旋女，莫空舞，
数唱此歌悟明主。

O Hun Dancing Girl

O Hun dancing girl, o Hun dancing girl,
Your hand the drum beat, your heart the strings twirl!
Moving light and slight, you raise up your sleeves,
Like thistledown that does flying snow whirl.
So tireless, you turn and turn, stirred the air;
So endless, you sway and sway, flowing there.
No race can compare with you in this world;
You swish like a cyclone, like a cart whirled.
The tune over, to the High Most you bow;
The High Most, so happy, smiles to you now.
O Hun dancing girl, the west is your land;
You have come east a long way through the sand.
Good dancers Mid Kingdom does also boast,
But in beauty and art you're uppermost.
The Heaven-Blessed reign might see change perchance
The palace ladies all learn how to dance.
Great True inside and Lushan An out there,
They can dance the best, best dancers to glare.
In Pear Garden Yang's favored, the blessed one;
And Yang adopts Lushan An as her son.
Lushan An's dance does dazzle the throne's eyes;
He does not doubt when the traitor's troops rise.
Yang has bewitched the throne all with her dance;
Yang slain at Mawei Slope, he's still in trance.
From now Heaven turns down and earth atop;
For fifty years it goes on without stop.
O Hun dancing girl, don't dance there in vain,
Sing loud and enlighten the throne again.

* Written in A.D. 809.
* The story of Jade Ring Yang and the Emperor Deepsire is told in the poem *Lasting Grief*.
* thistledown: the pappus of a thistle; the ripe silky fibers from the dry flower of a thistle, a metaphor for drifting or wandering.
* Mid Kingdom: alias China.
* Heaven-Blessed: one of the reign titles of Empire Deepsire, fifteen years from A.D. 742 to A.D. 756.
* Great True: Jade Ring's title, referring to Jade Ring (A.D. 719 – A.D. 756) or Jade Ring Yang, Deepsire the Emperor's Imperial Consort, a talented musician, one of the four beauties in Chinese history, the loveliest of the three thousand palace ladies of T'ang, ever accompanying the emperor's palanquin, singing and dancing to him.
* Lushan An: of the Kitan race, who distinguished himself in fighting against his own tribes, won the favor of Jade Ring and the confidence of Emperor Deepsire. His promotion being rapid, he was ennobled as a count, and made the governor of the border provinces of the north, where he held under command the best armies of the empire and nursed an inordinate ambition to own the empire. At one stage in their relationship, Jade Ring (Imperial Concubine Yang) made the rebel Lushan An her adopted son.
* Pear Garden: an operatic school established by Emperor Deepsire, where actors and actresses were trained, and the prototype of the modern Chinese drama was developed.
* Mawei Slope: the name of place west of Rising Peace, more than 30 miles from Long Peace, were Jade Ring and her cousin Kuochung Yang, the prime minister, were slain.

太行路

太行之路能摧车，
若比人心是坦途。
巫峡之水能覆舟，
若比人心是安流。
人心好恶苦不常，
好生毛羽恶生疮。
与君结发未五载，
岂期牛女为参商。
古称色衰相弃背，
当时美人犹怨悔。
何况如今鸾镜中，
妾颜未改君心改。
为君熏衣裳，
君闻兰麝不馨香。
为君盛容饰，
君看金翠无颜色。
行路难，难重陈。
人生莫作妇人身，
百年苦乐由他人。
行路难，难于山，险于水。
不独人间夫与妻，
近代君臣亦如此。
君不见左纳言，右纳史，
朝承恩，暮赐死。
行路难，不在水，不在山，
只在人情反覆间。

The Way to Mt. Great Go

The way to the Great Go can ruin a cart;
Compared with a man's heart, it's safe to start.
The Witch Gorge often overturns a boat;
Compared with a man's heart, it's safe to float.
A man's heart does change out and in;
A bird grows plumes or scabby skin.
Having been married for five years today,
Like Cowherd and Weaver, apart we stay.
As we read, when a lass grows old to fade,
She's aggrieved that in a void room she's laid.
Now the phoenix mirror I look into,
My face is the same, and your heart not true.
While your clothes I perfume,
From the musk you smell no balm.
While for you I dress up,
From the gold you see no charm.
The road is too hard, too hard for me to tell
When you are born. Don't be a woman born;
A woman's held by others, rose or thorn.
The road is too hard, harder than a mount, harder than a sea.
It's not just between man and wife alone;
It is the same between subject and throne.
Don't you espy the officials who censor, standing by,
Favored at dawn and at dusk made to die.
The road is too hard, hard not with a mount, hard not with a sea.
But with human feelings that change, too free.

* Mt. Great Go: Mt. T'aihang if transliterated, meandering on the border of Shanhsi,

Honan and Sha'anhsi, an important mountain range in East China and a geographic dividing line.
* Witch Gorge: One of the three gorges of the Long River, the other two being Big Pond Gorge and Westridge Gorge.
* Cowherd, the herding boy, Weaver's husband in the mythology of Cowherd and Weaver.
* Weaver: Weaver Maid, Vega, a fairy who loved Cowherd and was married to him in Chinese mythology. Weaver Maid was taken away and kept away from Cowherd by Queen Mother, and she stayed on the other side of the Silver River (the Milky Way) Queen Mother made with her hair pin.
* phoenix mirror: a mirror with a figure of a phoenix carved and cast on it.
* musk: a soft, reddish-brown powdery secretion of a penetrating odor, obtained from the preputial follicles of the male musk deer, used by perfumers and in medicine.

道州民

道州民，多侏儒，
长者不过三尺馀。
市作矮奴年进送，
号为道州任土贡。
任土贡，宁若斯？
不闻使人生别离，
老翁哭孙母哭儿！
一自阳城来守郡，
不进矮奴频诏问。
城云臣按六典书：
任土贡有不贡无。
道州水土所生者，
只有矮民无矮奴。
吾君感悟玺书下，
岁贡矮奴宜悉罢。
道州民，
老者幼者何欣欣！
父兄子弟始相保，
从此得作良人身。
道州民，
民到于今受其赐，
欲说使君先下泪。
仍恐儿孙忘使君，
生男多以阳为字。

The Dwarfs of Taochow

In Taochow, the seat, many dwarfs you meet;

The tallest one is no more than three feet;
They're picked out as slaves and sent to court,
A local product for fun or disport.
For fun or disport? Why play of this sort?
How many families are torn apart!
Gramps' cries are so keen, and grannies' so smart!
But the intendant called Shineton sends none,
Although court orders arrive one by one.
He replies he's checked law code the whole lot:
One should send what's produced, not what is not.
In Taochow here one may meet dwarfs indeed,
But they are short people, not slaves you need.
Then the Emperor issues a command;
The custom of sending dwarfs is now banned.
As the order's released,
In Taochow both old and young are so pleased.
All fathers and sons can rest at ease then,
And dwarfs are regarded as common men.
The folks of Taochow
Still 'member the favor done them you know.
When they speak of him, their tears first flow.
Lo, Shineton's into their sons' name combined
Lest they forget how Shine was to them kind.

* Taochow: today's Tao County, Hunan Province.
* dwarf: any human being, animal or plants that is much smaller than the usual size of its species.
* Shineton: Shineton (A.D. 753 – A.D. 805), from Summer County, Sha'anhsi, versed in classics and history, became an enteree in A.D. 783 and was appointed as Left Remonstrant. He was demoted to take the office as Prefect of Taochow in A.D. 789.

缚戎人

缚戎人,缚戎人,
耳穿面破驱入秦。
天子矜怜不忍杀,
诏徙东南吴与越。
黄衣小使录姓名,
领出长安乘递行。
身被金创面多瘠,
扶病徒行日一驿。
朝餐饥渴费杯盘,
夜卧腥臊污床席。
忽逢江水忆交河,
垂手齐声呜咽歌。
其中一虏语诸虏:
"尔苦非多我苦多!"
同伴行人因借问,
欲说喉中气愤愤。
自云乡贯本凉原,
大历年中没落蕃。
一落蕃中四十载,
遣着皮裘系毛带。
唯许正朝服汉仪,
敛衣整巾潜泪垂。
誓心密定归乡计,
不使蕃中妻子知。
暗思幸有残筋力,
更恐年衰归不得。
蕃候严兵鸟不飞,
脱身冒死奔逃归。

昼伏宵行经大漠，
云阴月黑风沙恶。
惊藏青冢寒草疏，
偷渡黄河夜冰薄。
忽闻汉军鼙鼓声，
路傍走出再拜迎。
游骑不听能汉语，
将军遂缚作蕃生。
配向东南卑湿地，
定无存恤空防备。
念此吞声仰诉天，
若为辛苦度残年。
凉原乡井不得见，
胡地妻儿虚弃捐。
没蕃被囚思汉土，
归汉被劫为蕃虏。
早知如此悔归来，
两地宁如一处苦！
缚戎人，
戎人之中我苦辛。
自古此冤应未有，
汉心汉语吐蕃身。

Jung Prisoners of War

Prisoners of war, prisoners of war,
Their ear pierced and tied, face broken, so sore.
They were driven to Long Peace, but not killed;
They were sent south so that land could be tilled.
A Yellow Robe registered their names and
They were led out of Long Peace, as was planned.

Covered with stab wounds, face pale like a ghost,
They trudged, hungry-thirsty, from post to post.
Without bowls or plates they were badly fed
And they slept on a filthy mat or bed.
Until one day they came upon a stream;
They knelt and sung a song, a sob or scream.
Now hark, among them there was one who said:
"Your don't suffer no much, I do instead."
So they asked him what was and what was not;
He answered, chest heaving, how he was caught.
He said he was from Coolton, a north town;
In the reign of Grand High he was put down.
For forty years he'd lived in Tubo there;
Only skins with a skin belt he could wear.
Hans were let to wear Han clothes for a day;
On that day his tears would drip all the way.
He swore and planned that back home he would go,
But would not let his alien wife and kids know.
Still alive, he saw no way to go back,
And he might fail as he grew old and slack.
The borders guarded, e'en birds could not fly,
But no matter how, he would have a try.
By day he slept, by night he walked the wild;
Heavy clouds, not moonlit, wind whirled sand piled.
He hid among tombs rampant with cold grass
And trod ice, the Yellow River to pass.
At last he heard Han drums and voice there rise;
He rose roadside to greet them and bow thrice.
The guards did not believe his Chinese tongue;
Thought as a spy, he was bound tight anon.
He was sent down south to damp areas now,

Not consoled but guarded, no matter how.
At this, he cried, his head raised to the sky;
He would wear out his last years by and by.
His homeland old he could ne'er see, ne'er e'er;
His Hun wife and kids were deserted there!
When first arrested, he missed Han his land;
Now in Han he was caught as a spy, and
He regretted he's managed to come back:
Suffering two racks is worse than one rack!
Prisoners of war,
Mid the Jungs I suffer the most, alack.
Who else has been wronged like this? There is none.
Chinese in, Chinese out, Tubo I'm one!

* Jung: referring to any of the ethnic minorities north of China.
* Long Peace: Ch'ang'an if transliterated, the capital of the T'ang Empire, with 1,000,000 inhabitants, the largest walled city ever built by man, and a cosmopolis swarming with all dignitaries from the world and the center of world religions, Buddhism, Confucianism, Wordism, Nestorianism, Zoroastrianism, and even Islamism represented by Saracens. Having evolved through the ages of Chough, Ch'in, Chin, Western Way, Later Chough, Sui and T'ang, it is now Hsi-an, West Peace literally, the capital of Sha'anhsi Province.
* Yellow Robe: a eunuch managing prisoners of war in yellow which denotes the lowest rank of eunuchs.
* Coolton: also known as Martial Might, Wuwei if transliterated, a prefectural city located in present-day Kansu Province, built by Emperor Martial of Han (156 B.C.-87 B.C.) to garrison the border, so named because Swift Huo defeated Huns and thus showed the martial might of the great Han Empire. It has been prosperous as the hub of the Silk Road and famous for wine brewage, hence styled Grape Wine Town.
* Grand High: the reign title of Emperor Tai (A.D. 768 – A.D. 779).
* Tubo: alias Tibet.
* the Yellow River: the second longest river in China, regarded as the cradle of Chinese civilization. It is 5,464 kilometers long, with a drainage area of 752,443 square

kilometers. As legend goes, the river derived from a yellow dragon that, couchant on Midland Plain, ate yellow soil, flooded crops, devoured people and stock, and was finally tamed by Great Worm, the First King of Hsia (21 B.C.- 16 B.C.).

骊宫高

高高骊山上有宫,
朱楼紫殿三四重。
迟迟兮春日,
玉甃暖兮温泉溢。
袅袅兮秋风,
山蝉鸣兮宫树红。
翠华不来岁月久,
墙有衣兮瓦有松。
吾君在位已五载,
何不一幸乎其中?
西去都门几多地,
吾君不游有深意。
一人出兮不容易,
六宫从兮百司备。
八十一车千万骑,
朝有宴饫暮有赐。
中人之产数百家,
未足充君一日费。
吾君修己人不知,
不自逸兮不自嬉。
吾君爱人人不识,
不伤财兮不伤力。
骊宫高兮高入云,
君之来兮为一身,
君之不来兮为万人。

Black Steed Palace

On Mt. Black Steed there's a palace so high,
Red towers and purple halls, three near, four by.
Late, o late, comes the spring sun;
A hot spring into the jade pool does run.
Sough, o sough, an autumn breeze;
The hill locusts shrill to the red wall trees.
The crown has not come for many a year;
Walls mossy, on the roof pine sprouts appear.
It's five years since His Majesty was crowned;
Why doesn't he descend to come around?
To the capital the palace not far,
Why don't we see the crown's Sedan car?
It's hard for an emperor to go out;
Ladies and servants must follow about.
Eighty-one carts and countless soldiers run;
Grand feasts and gifts given to everyone.
The monies of hundreds of households could
Not support the emperor's one day's food.
Now our emperor learns within the wall;
He seeks no comfort or pleasure at all.
Loving all folk though they don't know his love,
No money or labor he wastes above.
Black Steed Palace is so high, like the sun.
If our emperor comes, it's for his fun;
If he doesn't, it's for the world, for everyone.

* Black Steed Palace: a T'ang palace built on Mt. Black Steed.

* Mt. Black Steed: the mountain south of Lint'ung, an important offset of Mt. Ch'in Ridge, 1,302 meters above sea level, the location of the royal palace of Ch'in and tomb of Emperor First.

两朱阁

两朱阁,
南北相对起。
借问何人家?
贞元双帝子。
帝子吹箫双得仙,
五云飘飖飞上天。
第宅亭台不将去,
化为佛寺在人间。
妆阁伎楼何寂静,
柳似舞腰池似镜。
花落黄昏悄悄时,
不闻歌吹闻钟磬。
寺门敕榜金字书,
尼院佛庭宽有馀。
青苔明月多闲地,
比屋齐人无处居。
忆昨平阳宅初置,
吞并平人几家地?
仙去双双作梵宫,
渐恐人间尽为寺。

Two Red Towers

Two red towers there rise,
Facing each other eyes to eyes.
I'd like to ask who once lived there;
Two princesses of Right One fair.
They played the flute and became fairies there,

And rose to the five-hued clouds in the air.
Their houses were left after their rebirth
And became a Buddhist temple on the earth.
The dressing room for dancers then is void;
The willow's thin, the pool a glass deployed.
Flowers fall to the dusk, not saying a word;
No song is sung but a bell-chime is heard.
The plaque at gate is an imperial sign;
The nuns' rooms and the altar hall go fine.
For green moss and moonlight there is space wide;
But the folk have no homes to dwell outside;
When Princess of Peaceshine built her estate,
How many houses did she confiscate?
Now immortals, the two left their place here;
I'm afraid more such temples may appear.

* Two princesses of Right One: Emperor Virtue's two daughters, Right Solemn and Grand Solemn.
* Right One: Emperor Virtue's reign title, period lasting from A.D. 785 to A.D. 805.
* moss: a tiny, delicate green bryophytic plant growing on damp decaying wood, wet ground, humid rocks or trees, producing capsules which open by an operculum and contain spores. Under a poet's writing brush, it may arouse a poetic feeling or imagination.
* Princess of Peaceshine: Emperor Martial of Han's elder sister, notorious for luxury, a metaphor for Emperor Virtue's daughters.

涧底松

有松百尺大十围，
生在涧底寒且卑。
涧深山险人路绝，
老死不逢工度之。
天子明堂欠梁木，
此求彼有两不知。
谁谕苍苍造物意，
但与之材不与地。
金张世禄原宪贫，
牛衣寒贱貂蝉贵。
貂蝉与牛衣，
高下虽有殊。
高者未必贤，
下者未必愚。
君不见沉沉海底生珊瑚，
历历天上种白榆。

Pines in the Dale

Pines one hundred feet tall, ten arms around,
Grow in the dale low and cold down below.
The dale deep, dangerous, and no way found,
No carpenter e'er comes for timber, no.
A palace being built need beams and wood;
No one knows that there are pines here, so good.
Who can fathom God's will and offer grace,
Using proper things in their proper place?
The rich, the sage are of a different tier;

A herd's coat is cheep, a crown pearl is dear.
A herd's coat there, a crown pearl here,
One is low and cheep, one is high and dear.
The high may not be upraised;
The low may not be debased.
Don't you espy in the depth of the ocean corals grow,
High above in the heaven poplars show?

* pine: any of a genus (*Pinus*) of evergreen trees of the pine family, a cone-bearing tree having bundles of two to five needle-shaped leaves growing in clusters, an important image in Chinese literature, a symbol of rectitude, longevity and so on.
* coral: the hard, stony skeleton secreted by certain marine polyps and often deposited in extensive masses forming reefs and atolls in tropical seas.
* poplar: any of a genus (*Populus*) of dioecious trees and bushes of the willow family, widely distributed in the northern hemisphere.

牡丹芳

牡丹芳，牡丹芳，
黄金蕊绽红玉房。
千片赤英霞烂烂，
百枝绛点灯煌煌。
照地初开锦绣段，
当风不结兰麝囊。
仙人琪树白无色，
王母桃花小不香。
宿露轻盈泛紫艳，
朝阳照耀生红光。
红紫二色间深浅，
向背万态随低昂。
映叶多情隐羞面，
卧丛无力含醉妆。
低娇笑容疑掩口，
凝思怨人如断肠。
秾姿贵彩信奇绝，
杂卉乱花无比方。
石竹金钱何细碎，
芙蓉芍药苦寻常。
遂使王公与卿士，
游花冠盖日相望。
庳车软舆贵公主，
香衫细马豪家郎。
卫公宅静闭东院，
西明寺深开北廊。
戏蝶双舞看人久，
残莺一声春日长。

共愁日照芳难驻，
仍张帐幕垂阴凉。
花开花落二十日，
一城之人皆若狂。
三代以还文胜质，
人心重华不重实。
重华直至牡丹芳，
其来有渐非今日。
元和天子忧农桑，
恤下动天天降祥。
去岁嘉禾生九穗，
田中寂寞无人至。
今年瑞麦分两岐，
君心独喜无人知。
无人知，可叹息。
我愿暂求造化力，
减却牡丹妖艳色。
少回卿士爱花心，
同似吾君忧稼穑。

O Peony So Fine

They at once spread out a shining brocade;
Their perfume wafts as if from a cascade;
The beauties in Fairyland are outshone;
Queen Mother's peach is only a small one.
O peony so fine, o peony so fine;
Golden stamens and pollen petals shine.
Thousands of blossoms do burst into blaze;
Hundreds of lanterns glorious give off rays.
At night these blooms with dew at their best flush;

At dawn the sun does rise as if to blush.
Crimson and purple, one deep, the other light;
Sapphire and yellow, some dim, the other bright.
Leaves wearing their brightest hue feel so shy;
Stems drooping low may have drunk their wine dry.
Alluring lips parted laugh at the bloom;
A musing belle annoyed complains in gloom.
A luxury they are, of the best grade;
Insignificant, all other flowers fade.
Carnations and tulips are dwarfed so much;
Lotuses and roses are lowered as such.
Each day great officials come for the show;
Carriage after carriage make a great flow.
Cars and sedans come and go without cease,
Holding princes and princesses at ease.
Lord Watch's house is calm, east yard closed so right;
West Bright Fane is deep, north gate oped to light.
The butterfly dance attracts one for long;
Orioles' cry is spring's prolonging song.
We're all sad we can't keep the sunlit hours;
Still we will put up tents as cooling bowers.
For twenty days on, flowers bloom and flowers fall;
The whole town run about, crazy for all.
Since Three Kings, splendor has had more appeal;
People stress on form instead of what's real.
So peonies have come to win everyone;
Not just today the customs have begun.
The One Cord Emperor cares about grain;
Thus Heaven blesses all so they can gain.
The grain budded with many ears last year;
The fields so deserted, no one would veer.

  This year grain split in two, the output rose;
  The emperor rejoiced, yet no one knows.
  No one knows, how sad; what a sigh, like mad.
  May I be blessed with great creating power
  So that I'll decolor peonies' best flower.
  Gentlemen, do from flower-viewing refrain;
  Like our emperor, take more care of grain.

* peony: any of a genus of perennial, often double-flowered, plants of the peony family, with large pink, yellow, red, or white showy flowers.
* Fairyland: a legendary ideal abode for immortals, sometimes thought of as being in the middle of East Sea, sometimes high above in the sky.
* Queen Mother: referring to Mother West, a sovereign goddess living on Mt. Queen in Chinese myths. She was originally described as human-bodied, tiger-toothed, leopard-tailed and hoopoe-haired, regarded as a goddess in charge of women protection, marriage and procreation, and longevity. According to *Sir Lush*, with the Word, Queen Mother sat on Mt. Young Broad.
* carnation: a popular garden and greenhouse plant of the pink family, usually with white, pink, or red double flowers that smell like cloves.
* tulip: any of various bulb plants of the lily family, mostly spring-blooming, with long, broad, pointed leaves, and usually, a single, large, cup-shaped, variously colored flower.
* lotus: one of the various plants of the waterlily family, noted for their large floating leaves and showy flowers, an important image in Chinese culture; in most cases it is associated with Buddhism, for example, Pai Li has various names, one of which is Green Lotus Buddhist.
* rose: any of a genus of shrubs of the rose family, characteristically with prickly stems, alternate compound leaves, and five-parted, usually fragrant flowers of red, pink, white, yellow, etc., having many stamens. It is often used as a metaphor for beauty or love.
* Lord Watch: Ching Li (A.D. 571 – A.D. 649), the First General of T'ang, granted Marquis of Watch.
* West Bright Fane: a resort for peony shows in the T'ang dynasty.
* butterfly: any of various families of lepidopteran insects active in the day-time, having a sucking mouthpart, slender body, ropelike, knobbed antennae, and four broad,

usually brightly colored, membraneous wings.
* oriole: golden oriole, one of the family of passerine birds, which looks bright yellow with contrasting black wings and sings beautiful songs.
* Three Kings: a metonymy for the three dynasties, i.e., Hsia, Shang, and Chough.
* the One Cord Emperor: referring to Emperor Statute (Hsienchung if transliterated), One Cord being his reign title, from A.D. 805 to A.D. 820. During One Cord, T'ang became prosperous again, hence One Cord Resurgence.

红线毯

红线毯，
择茧缲丝清水煮，
拣丝练线红蓝染。
染为红线红于蓝，
织作披香殿上毯。
披香殿广十丈馀，
红线织成可殿铺。
彩丝茸茸香拂拂，
线软花虚不胜物。
美人踏上歌舞来，
罗袜绣鞋随步没。
太原毯涩毳缕硬，
蜀都褥薄锦花冷。
不如此毯温且柔，
年年十月来宣州。
宣城太守加样织，
自谓为臣能竭力。
百夫同担进宫中，
线厚丝多卷不得。
宣城太守知不知？
一丈毯，
千两丝！
地不知寒人要暖，
少夺人衣作地衣。

The Red Silk Carpet

The Red Silk Carpet,

From fine cocoons and in clean water boiled,
The silk dyed blue or red is reeled and coiled.
When red silk's ready, it is like flowers red;
A carpet is made and on Balm Hall spread.
Balm Hall is more than thirty meters wide;
The red carpet is spread from side to side.
The colored softer than wool is perfumed,
Its flowery patterns true to life assumed.
When palace beauties have come to the ball,
Their silk socks and 'broidered shoes please the hall.
Great Plain carpets look stubby and not fine;
Silkton carpets look flowery and do shine;
Lo and behold, that carpet's soft and sheer,
Sent all the way from Hsuan year after year.
Hsuan's prefect did work hard for carpets rare,
Saying that he'd no more energy to spare.
A hundred bore the carpet to the hall,
Too huge that they could not roll it at all.
Does the prefect of Hsuan know this or not.
For ten feet to be wrought,
A thousand ounces brought.
The earth does not feel cold but all men do;
They're robbed of silk for carpets red or blue!

* cocoon: the silky or fibrous case which the larvae of certain insects spin about themselves for shelter during the pupa stage.
* silk: the fine, soft, shiny fiber produced by silk worms to form their cocoons, and the thread or fabric made from this fibre is used as material for clothing. And it can be any clothing made of silk.
* Great Plain: referring to T'aiyüan if transliterated, the place where the first emperor of T'ang, Yüan Li, and the second emperor, Shimin Li, i.e. Yüan Li's son, were stationed in the Sui dynasty. As Great Plain was once called T'ang, T'ang was adopted

as the name of the T'ang Empire.

* Silkton: alias Ch'engtu, now the capital of Ssuch'uan Province, a city that has been prosperous with fine silk for thousands of years.
* Hsuan: an ancient town in present-day Hsuan, Anhui Province, a county instituted in the early years of the Ch'in Emperor under the Prefecture of Redshine. It became a prefecture in A.D. 281 during the Chin dynasty. It is well known for rich historical legacies, and best remembered for its high-quality rice paper.

杜陵叟

杜陵叟，杜陵居，
岁种薄田一顷馀。
三月无雨旱风起，
麦苗不秀多黄死。
九月降霜秋早寒，
禾穗未熟皆青干。
长吏明知不申破，
急敛暴征求考课。
典桑卖地纳官租，
明年衣食将何如？
剥我身上帛，
夺我口中粟。
虐人害物即豺狼，
何必钩爪锯牙食人肉？
不知何人奏皇帝，
帝心恻隐知人弊。
白麻纸上书德音，
京畿尽放今年税。
昨日里胥方到门，
手持敕牒榜乡村。
十家租税九家毕，
虚受吾君蠲免恩。

The Old Man of Birchleaf Hill

Birchleaf Man lives on Birchleaf Hill；
He's more than an acre of land to till.
Then comes a spring drought there, a season dry

Three months of hot winds blow wheat shoots to die;
The ninth moon there come frosts, it getting cold;
The crops are still green, not yet turning gold.
The officials know this but don't report,
But collect all taxes and all extort.
Mulberry farm sold, field pawned, taxes to pay
Where will food or clothes come from, anyway?
Clothes are from his back stripped, not stopped;
Food is from his mouth grabbed, all dropped.
They're wolves coveting people's flesh and blood;
Why tear them with teeth and claws and throw their bones, thud?
Someone does make a report to the throne
And the emperor has his goodness shown.
He sends down a rescript drawn on hemp white
To have district taxes remitted, right!
Yesterday the local official came to each door,
Rescript in hand, shouting: Tax there's no more.
Of ten households nine have paid the whole lot;
They have received imperial grace for nought.

* Birchleaf Hill: known as Birchleaf Pear Ridge formally — 10 kilometers from Wannien County, in today's Hsi-an, Sha'anhsi Province.
* wheat: a grain yielding an edible flour, the annual product of a cereal grass (genus *Triticum*), introduced to China from West Asia more than 4,000 years ago, used as a staple food in China and most of the world. In its importance to consumers, it is second only to rice.
* mulberry: the edible, berry-like juicy fruit of a tree (genus *Morus*) whose leaves are valued for silkworm culture, and the tree itself.
* wolf: a large carnivorous mammal related to the dog, regarded as ravenous, cruel, or rapacious, a metaphor for an invader or lecher in Chinese culture.

缭　绫

缭绫缭绫何所似？
不似罗绡与纨绮。
应似天台山上明月前，
四十五尺瀑布泉。
中有文章又奇绝，
地铺白烟花簇雪。
织者何人衣者谁？
越溪寒女汉宫姬。
去年中使宣口敕，
天上取样人间织。
织为云外秋雁行，
染作江南春水色。
广裁衫袖长制裙，
金斗熨波刀剪纹。
异彩奇文相隐映，
转侧看花花不定。
昭阳舞人恩正深，
春衣一对值千金。
汗沾粉污不再着，
曳土踏泥无惜心。
缭绫织成费功绩，
莫比寻常缯与帛。
丝细缲多女手疼，
扎扎千声不盈尺。
昭阳殿里歌舞人，
若见织时应也惜。

Twine Silk

Twine silk, o twine silk, what does it look like?
Not like chiffon, satin, damask or gauze.
It'd be like the moon o'er Mt. Sky Altar,
Where the forty-five high waterfall pours.
There are figures, patterns and designs bright,
Beneath them blossoms of snow and smoke white.
Who's the silk weaving? who will the silk wear?
The Yüeh Stream girl, the palace lady fair.
Last year an order came from the Most High
For maids to weave with samples from the sky.
Weaving silk with clouded wild geese in flight;
Dyed with southern spring water hue so bright.
The long is made into sleeves, the short, skirts;
Ironed will be waves and cut off will be spurts.
The colors and the lines each to each shine;
Flowers are looked at and flowers are turning fine.
The dancer in Glare Hall His eyes behold;
The twin gowns are worth a chest of gold.
If stained with sweat or dirt, it's thrown anon
Trodden or trampled, it's cared by no one.
Weaving such twine silk takes much force and pain
Don't compare it with textiles having grain.
Her hands hurt dressing piles of cocoons boiled,
Tic-tacking for hours, she's no much silk coiled.
Palace dancers, if you see how it's done
You'll cherish the silk as the weaving one.

* chiffon: a sheer, lightweight fabric of silk, nylon, etc.

* satin: a fabric of silk or other similar material having a smooth finish, glossy on the face and dull on the back.
* damask: a durable, lustrous, reversible fabric as of silk or linen, in figured weave, used for table linen, upholstery, etc.
* the moon: the planet of the earth, which appears at night and gives off shining silvery light, an image of purity and solitude in Chinese culture.
* Mt. Sky Altar: alias Mt. Heaven Terrace, a mountain in Chechiang Province.
* silk: the fine, soft, shiny fiber produced by silk worms to form their cocoons, and the thread or fabric made from this fibre is used as material for clothing. And it can be any clothing made of silk.
* the Yüeh Stream: the Yüeh River, probably referring to the O Ts'ao River, the largest branch of the Ch'ient'ang River.
* wild goose: an undomesticated goose that is caring and responsible, taken as a symbol of benevolence, righteousness, good manner, wisdom, and faith in Chinese culture.
* cocoon: the silky or fibrous case which the larvae of certain insects spin about themselves for shelter during the pupa stage.

卖炭翁

卖炭翁,
伐薪烧炭南山中。
满面尘灰烟火色,
两鬓苍苍十指黑。
卖炭得钱何所营?
身上衣裳口中食。
可怜身上衣正单,
心忧炭贱愿天寒。
夜来城外一尺雪,
晓驾炭车辗冰辙。
牛困人饥日已高,
市南门外泥中歇。
翩翩两骑来是谁?
黄衣使者白衫儿。
手把文书口称敕,
回车叱牛牵向北。
一车炭,千馀斤,
宫使驱将惜不得。
半匹红绡一丈绫,
系向牛头充炭直。

The Charcoal Gray Hair

The charcoal Gray Hair,
He fells trees for charcoal in south hills there.
He's dirty with dust and smoke, front or back;
His sideburns gray and his fingers all black.
What will he do with the money he earns?

Food, clothing, and all those daily concerns.
So poor, the garment he wears is so thin;
For higher price, he hopes winter to set in.
Outside the wall at night, a foot of snow,
At dawn he drives his cart down ice to go.
So tired, the sun high, and the ox so pressed,
Outside South Gate, in snow and slush he'll rest.
Lo, riders trotting up, who are they guessed?
A herald in gold and a boy white dressed.
Decree in hand, "An edict here", they shout;
To north they turn the ox and cart about.
A cart of charcoal half a ton does weigh;
What can he do now they take it away?
A foot of red silk, and damask gauze spread,
The price for charcoal, tied to the ox's head.

* charcoal: a porous amorphous form of carbon produced by destructive distillation of wood or other organic matter and used as firewood or for heating.
* ox: any of several bovid ruminants as cattle, buffaloes, bison, gaur, and yaks; especially a domesticated bull (*Bos taurus*), used as a draft animal, a symbol of diligence in Chinese culture.
* silk: the fine, soft, shiny fiber produced by silk worms to form their cocoons, and the thread or fabric made from this fibre is used as material for clothing. And it can be any clothing made of silk.
* damask: a durable, lustrous, reversible fabric as of silk or linen, in figured weave, used for table linen, upholstery, etc.

官　牛

官牛官牛驾官车，
浐水岸边般载沙。
一石沙，几斤重？
朝载暮载将何用？
载向五门官道西，
绿槐阴下铺沙堤。
昨来新拜右丞相，
恐怕泥涂污马蹄。
右丞相，
马蹄踏沙虽净洁，
牛领牵车欲流血。
右丞相，
但能济人治国调阴阳，
官牛领穿亦无妨。

The Official Ox

Official oxen official carts draw,
Carrying the Ts'an's sand, carrying more.
A picul of sand, what is the weight?
What's the use, so sent, for things small or great?
Carried to Five Gates, west of the Broad Way
To build the dyke where the locust trees sway.
Yesterday came a new councilor curt;
He feared that his horse's hooves might get dirt.
O Right Minister,
Treading on sand the hooves will remain clean;
Hauling the carts the oxen bleed, so keen.

O Right Minister,
If you do well and regulate our state,
It doesn't matter if the oxen grate.

* the Ts'an: the Ts'an River, originating from the Ch'in Ridge southwest of Blue Field and flowing into the Pa River east of Long Peace.
* picul: a unit of weight, a hundred catties or 50 kilograms.
* Five Gates: five of the twelve gates of Long Peace.
* locust tree: a spiny tree of the pea family, having long pendulous racemes of fragrant edible white flowers.
* Right Minister: equivalent to Prime Minister, and Left Minister equivalent to Deputy Prime Minister.

紫毫笔

紫毫笔，
尖如锥兮利如刀。
江南石上有老兔，
吃竹饮泉生紫毫。
宣城之人采为笔，
千万毛中拣一毫。
毫虽轻，
功甚重。
管勒工名充岁贡，
君兮臣兮勿轻用。
勿轻用，
将何如？
愿赐东西府御史，
愿颁左右台起居。
搦管趋入黄金阙，
抽毫立在白玉除。
臣有奸邪正笴奏，
君有动言直笔书。
起居郎，
侍御史，
尔知紫毫不易致。
每岁宣城进笔时，
紫毫之价如金贵。
慎勿空将弹失仪，
慎勿空将录制词。

The Purple Hair Brush

The Purple hair brush,
Pointed like an awl, sharp as a knife, hush;
Hares hide amidst rocks in the south down there,
Eating bamboo, drinking spring, growing purple hair.
Folks in Hsuan pluck it for a writing tool;
One's picked out, out of a million by rule.
A hair is so light;
The worth is not slight.
The brushes sent as tribute to the court,
Lord and peers, treat them not as a cheap sort.
Not as a cheap sort,
Used for what purport?
Censorate, historians, use them to write;
Ministers, secretaries, use them to fight.
Holding the brush, you enter the hall grand;
Twirling the hair, on a jade step you stand.
Those evil and crafty you should chastise
His Majesty, when loose, you should advise.
Recorders, do rise,
Attendants, be wise,
You know it's hard to find a brush so nice.
When brushes are sent here from Huan each year
The price of purple hair is high, so dear.
Pray use it to admonish the Most High;
Pray use it to note what comes and goes by.

* Written in Long Peace in the year A.D. 809.
* hare: a rodent (genus *Lepus*) with cleft upper lip, long ears, and long hind legs —

characterized by its timidity and swiftness, habitating woodland, farmland or grassland.
* the south: It literally means "South of the Yangtze River" but in fact refers to today's Chiangsu and Chechiang provinces.
* bamboo: a tall, tree-like or shrubby grass in tropical and semi-tropical regions.
* Hsuan: an ancient town, especially famous for its paper made of ebony wood, in present-day Hsuan, Anhui Province.

隋堤柳

隋堤柳，
岁久年深尽衰朽。
风飘飘兮雨萧萧，
三株两株汴河口。
老枝病叶愁杀人，
曾经大业年中春。
大业年中炀天子，
种柳成行夹流水。
西自黄河东至淮，
绿影一千三百里。
大业末年春暮月，
柳色如烟絮如雪。
南幸江都恣佚游，
应将此柳系龙舟。
紫髯郎将护锦缆，
青娥御史直迷楼。
海内财力此时竭，
舟中歌笑何日休？
上荒下困势不久，
宗社之危如缀旒。
炀天子，
自言福祚长无穷，
岂知皇子封酅公。
龙舟未过彭城阁，
义旗已入长安宫。
萧墙祸生人事变，
晏驾不得归秦中。
土坟数尺何处葬？

吴公台下多悲风。
二百年来汴河路，
沙草和烟朝复暮。
后王何以鉴前王？
请看隋堤亡国树。

Sui Dyke Willows Gray

Sui Dyke willows gray,
So old, they have now fallen to decay.
The wind blows, o the rain does sough and sough;
Three trees or two on the Pien River bow.
The old branches, the sick leaves, what sad trees!
Planted in Sui, they once enjoyed spring breeze.
In the great reign of Emperor Melt Fine;
On both banks willows were planted to line.
From the Yellow to the Huai all the way,
Green shades were cast four hundred miles to fay.
The end of the reign saw a late spring show;
The green hue was like mist, catkins like snow.
The Lord went south to Yangchow to tour free;
He'd have his dragon barge tied to the tree.
His generals were pulling silk hawsers there;
His censors were enjoying ladies fair.
All treasuries were exhausted, hard pressed;
When would dances and songs in the barge rest?
Squander up and poverty down won't last;
Danger will come to the empire so fast.
Emperor Melt Fine,
He thought his blessing would go without bound,
So then His prince was as Duke of Hsieh crowned.

Before his dragon barge passed P'eng on route,
Rebels stormed Long Peace and did Long Peace loot.
A disaster fell, all changed in the west;
He couldn't go back, and all were depressed.
Where to bury Him? There is a small tomb.
Under Lord Wu's Mound, a wind sighed in gloom.
For two hundred years Pien Dyke has there stayed,
Seeing sedge and smoke and all those who wade.
How could a later emperor still be?
Please look at Sui Dyke and the fallen tree.

* willow: any of a large genus of shrubs and trees related to the poplars, having generally narrow leaves, smooth branches, and often long, slender, pliant, and sometimes pendent branchlets, a symbol of farewell or nostalgia in Chinese culture. The best image is in *Vetch We Pick*, a verse in *The Book of Songs*, which reads like this: When we left long ago, / The willows waved adieu. / Now back to our home town, / We meet snow falling down.
* the Pien River: an ancient river that originated from Hsingshine and flowed into the Ssu River in P'eng.
* Sui: the Sui dynasty (A.D. 581 – A.D. 619), a transitional period between the Northern and Southern Dynasties period and the great T'ang dynasty. In February 581, Emperor Calm of Northern Chough abdicated and handed his throne over to Chien Yang, the first emperor of Sui, who reunified China.
* Emperor Melt Fine: Kuang Yang (A.D. 569 – A.D. 618) the second emperor of Sui, one of the most famous emperors in Chinese history.
* the Yellow: the Yellow River, the second longest river in China, regarded as the cradle of Chinese civilization. It is 5,464 kilometers long, with a drainage area of 752,443 square kilometers. As legend goes, the river derived from a yellow dragon that, couchant on Midland Plain, ate yellow soil, flooded crops, devoured people and stock, and was finally tamed by Great Worm, the First King of Hsia (21 B.C.– 16 B.C.).
* the Huai: referring to the River Huai, one of the seven rivers in China, between the Long River and the Yellow River, 1,000 kilometers long.
* catkin: a deciduous scaly spike of flowers, as in the willow, an image of helpless drifting or wandering in Chinese literature.

* Yangchow: an important city in today's Chiangsu Province, the greatest port in China and the centre of luxury trades in the T'ang dynasty.
* P'eng: today's Hsuchow, Chiangsu Province.
* Long Peace: Ch'ang'an if transliterated, the metropolis of gold, the capital of the T'ang Empire, with 1,000,000 inhabitants, the largest walled city ever built by man, and now the capital of today's Sha'anhsi Province. Long Peace saw the wonder of Chinese civilization that reached the pinnacle of brilliance in Emperor Deepsire's reign.
* Lord Wu's Mound: in Yangchow, built by Sung in the Southern Dynasties, as a vantage point for arrow shooting.

古冢狐

古冢狐，妖且老，
化为妇人颜色好。
头变云鬟面变妆，
大尾曳作长红裳。
徐徐行傍荒村路，
日欲暮时人静处。
或歌或舞或悲啼，
翠眉不举花颜低。
忽然一笑千万态，
见者十人八九迷。
假色迷人犹若是，
真色迷人应过此。
彼真此假俱迷人，
人心恶假贵重真。
狐假女妖害犹浅，
一朝一夕迷人眼。
女为狐媚害即深，
日长月长溺人心。
何况褒妲之色善蛊惑，
能丧人家覆人国。
君看为害浅深间，
岂将假色同真色？

The Ancient Tomb Fox

The ancient tomb fox, so sly and so old,
Has turned into a lovely belle, behold.
Her hair-do high, her face powdered, well drawn,

Her tail's become the train of a red gown.
She tiptoes and walks the deserted trail;
The dusk sees calmness in the burg prevail.
She sings and dances or sadly she cries;
She lowers her painted brows and drops her eyes.
She bursts to smile like a thousand flowers dance;
Most of those who see her are lost in trance.
The false beauty lures one like real as much;
A real beauty can't lure any as such.
That is real, this is false, but both appeal;
Human hearts evil, we'd cherish the real.
The fox in a belle's skin is but a lie,
But for one day or two, cheating your eye.
A belle in a fox's skin harms the whole;
Day in day out, she does extract your soul.
Remember Pao Ssu and Tachi, beauties of the first rate,
They could kill a house and upturn a state.
The harm can be a dungeon or a hell;
Don't mix a false beauty with a real belle.

* Pao Ssu: an imperial concubine of King Dark of Chough (? - 771 B.C.). As is recorded, in order to please Pao Ssu, King Dark ignited the beacons, which were used as an alarm to apprise of enemies' coming, to fool the vassal lords. Once the enemies really attacked, King Dark ignited the beacons again, but nobody believed him as he had fooled them too many times before. So Chough collapsed and King Dark was killed.
* Tachi: an imperial concubine of King Chow (1075 B.C.- 1046 B.C.), the last emperor of Shang. It is said that King Chow spent too much time with Tachi and neglected government affairs, therefore, Shang was overthrown by Chough.

黑潭龙

黑潭水深黑如墨,
传有神龙人不识。
潭上驾屋官立祠,
龙不能神人神之。
丰凶水旱与疾疫,
乡里皆言龙所为。
家家养豚漉清酒,
朝祈暮赛依巫口。
神之来兮风飘飘,
纸钱动兮锦伞摇。
神之去兮风亦静,
香火灭兮杯盆冷。
肉堆潭岸石,
酒泼庙前草。
不知龙神飨几多,
林鼠山狐长醉饱。
狐何幸?
豚何辜?
年年杀豚将喂狐,
狐假龙神食豚尽,
九重泉底龙知无?

The Black Pool Dragon

The black pool is deep, black like inky clay;
There lives a dragon there as all folk say.
The pool sees an official temple stand;
The dragon's no god, made god of the land.

When floods, droughts or diseases wildly run,
All say this is what the dragon has done.
Those living nearby rear pigs and brew wine.
And as told by witches, pray to the shrine.
As wind blows, they see Dragon God alight!
From paper money they burn leap flames bright.
Dragon God is gone, wind is gone, behold!
Incense dying out, bowls, basins are cold.
Meat piled up are left on the stone,
Wine spilled on grass, cups there o'er thrown.
Who knows for how long this dragon has dined?
Rats and foxes have long dined here we find.
How blessed, foxes shine!
How sad, doomed are swine!
Each year swine are killed to feed foxes fine.
Instead of Dragon God, foxes eat all
Does the dragon down the pool know at all?

* dragon: a fabulous serpent-like giant winged animal that can change its girth and length, a symbol of benevolence and sovereignty in Chinese culture while a black or black pool dragon has a negative image.
* Dragon God: the imaginary God ruling dragons.
* swine: any of a family of omnivorous, artiodactylous mammals with a bristly coat and elongated, flexible snout, especially a domesticated pig or a hog.
* fox: a burrowing canine mammal (genus *Vulpes*) having a long pointed muzzle and a long bushy tail, commonly reddish-brown in color, characterized by its cunning.

天可度

天可度，
地可量，
唯有人心不可防。
但见丹诚赤如血，
谁知伪言巧似簧。
劝君掩鼻君莫掩，
使君夫妇为参商。
劝君掇蜂君莫掇，
使君父子成豺狼。
海底鱼兮天上鸟，
高可射兮深可钓。
唯有人心相对时，
咫尺之间不能料。
君不见李义府之辈笑欣欣，
笑中有刀潜杀人。
阴阳神变皆可测，
不测人间笑是瞋。

We Can Gauge the Earth

We can gauge the earth;
We can gauge the blue,
But a human heart we can never do.
We can see one's faithfulness like blood run;
But how can we distinguish a glib tongue?
Advised to "cover your nose", you don't do,
Which may take your husband away from you.
Advised to stir up bees, you should not;

Which may bring father and son troubles hot.
There're fish in the sea, and birds in the sky;
You can fish for what's deep and shoot what's high.
But men, who stand eye to eye, face to face,
You can't be sure of e'en in a small space.
Don't you espy those who, like Premier Li, smirk and smile
Hide a knife under the cover of guile.
The law of nature one can estimate;
How can you judge a smile that covers hate?

* This poem contains references to various incidents of slander well known at the time.
* Cover your nose: referring to an imperial concubine who was told by a jealous colleague that the Emperor did not like her nose and that she should cover it with her hand when in his presence. The Emperor seeing her do this asked the jealous colleague the reason. She said that it was because the concubine found his body odour objectionable. This led to serious consequences for the concubine and to her rival gaining imperial favour.
* Premier Li: referring to Linfu Li (A.D. 683 – A.D. 753), a corrupt prime minister.

秦吉了

秦吉了,
出南中,
彩毛青黑花颈红。
耳聪心慧舌端巧,
鸟语人言无不通。
昨日长爪鸢,
今朝大嘴乌。
鸢捎乳燕一窠覆,
乌啄母鸡双眼枯。
鸡号堕地燕惊去,
然后拾卵攫其雏。
岂无雕与鹗?
嗉中肉饱不肯搏。
亦有鸾鹤群,
闲立扬高如不闻。
秦吉了,
人云尔是能言鸟,
岂不见鸡燕之冤苦?
吾闻凤凰百鸟主,
尔竟不为凤凰之前致一言,
安用噪噪闲言语。

The Grackle

The grackle so grand
Is from Southern Land,
Plumes glossy, black, round its neck a red band.
Its ears acute, tongue clever and brain smart,

It can speak languages from every part.

Yesterday a hawk with sharp claws,

Today a big-mouthed crow that caws!

The hawk seized and tore a swallow's nest then;

The crow pecked out the two eyes of a hen.

The hen squawked and away the swallows fled,

The eggs eaten, the chicks pecked off their head.

No vulture or owl there to kill?

Stuffed to their fill, they won't fight with their bill.

Also a flock of storks nearby

Watch what's happening and off they fly.

O grackle so grand,

They all say you speak all tongues of the land,

Don't you see the sufferance hens and swallows stand?

They say the phoenix is Lord of all birds;

Why don't you go to him and on their behalf use kind words?

Why do you sit there chattering like turds?

* grackle: a starling like bird, usually shining and sable-black with a yellow stripe around the neck, which can imitate human speech and singing. It is used as a metaphor for a remonstrant in this poem.
* hawk: a diurnal bird of prey, notable for keen sight and strong flight, usually used as a metaphor for one who takes military means in contrast with a dove, one who tries to find peaceful solutions.
* swallow: a passerine bird, with short broad, depressed bill, long pointed wings, and forked tail, noted for fleeting flight and migratory habits. In Chinese culture, swallows are welcome to live with a family with their nest on a beam of a sitting room.
* crow: an omnivorous, raucous, oscine bird of the genus *Corvus*, with glossy black plumage. It is regarded as an ominous bird, a metaphor for death because it is a scavenger, feeding on carrion. It is a common image in Chinese literature, which can be found in *The Book of Songs* compiled 2,500 years ago: "Crows are all black, it's said, / So as foxes are red."
* vulture: a large bird of prey, related to the eagles, hawks, and falcons, having the

head and neck naked or partly naked, feeding mostly on carrion.
* owl: a predatory nocturnal bird, having large eyes and head, short, sharply hooked bill, long powerful claws, and a circular facial disk of radiating feathers, regarded as ominous in Chinese culture.
* stork: any of a family of large, long-legged wading birds having a long neck and bill.
* phoenix: In Chinese myths, phoenixes, auspicious birds, unlike ordinary ones, only perch on parasol trees, and only eat bamboo shoots and pearly stone.

采诗官

采诗官，
采诗听歌导人言。
言者无罪闻者诫，
下流上通上下泰。
周灭秦兴至隋氏，
十代采诗官不置。
郊庙登歌赞君美，
乐府艳词悦君意。
若求兴谕规刺言，
万句千章无一字。
不是章句无规刺，
渐及朝廷绝讽议。
净臣杜口为冗员，
谏鼓高悬作虚器。
一人负扆常端默，
百辟入门两自媚。
夕郎所贺皆德音，
春官每奏唯祥瑞。
君之堂兮千里远，
君之门兮九重閟。
君耳唯闻堂上言，
君眼不见门前事。
贪吏害民无所忌，
奸臣蔽君无所畏。
君不见厉王胡亥之末年，
群臣有利君无利。
君兮君兮愿听此，
欲开壅蔽达人情，

先向歌诗求讽刺。

The Folk Song Scribe

Folk song scribe,
Listen to folks sing and how they describe.
A speaker bears no blame, a hearer learns;
A lower view reaches high and downward turns.
From Chough to Ch'in and Sui no more such air,
And in ten dynasties no post laid there.
All songs are eulogies, all are the same;
At altars, shrines, fanes all praise Most High's name.
For sneers, satires, criticisms, or confines,
You can find one word in ten thousand lines.
It is not that the folks do not give advice,
But that the court has banned all that is wise.
Remonstrants stand and their mouths closed remain
The warning drum stays hung high, all in vain.
Ministers face the throne, in silence mere;
Courtiers pour in, all to flatter and cheer.
Attendants all warm compliments convey;
Rite officers all auspices display.
The emperor's hall is one thousand miles far;
The emperor's doors close, closed tight they are!
The emperor hears what is from the court;
The emperor sees not a truth report.
Corrupt ministers harm the folks and cheer;
Crafty traitors blind the crown without fear.
Don't you espy at the end of King Strict's or Hai Hu's reign
All courtiers but the throne had much to gain?
O Your Majesty, please listen to me:

All barriers should go, all speech should be free;
Collect songs where you can hear, you can see.

* folk song scribe: a member of the office in charge of poetry collection from the folk, instituted in the Chough dynasty. Most poems in *The Book of Songs* were collected in this way.
* Chough: the State of Chough (1046 B.C.- 256 B.C.), the third kingdom in Chinese history, comprising Western Chough and Eastern Chough.
* Ch'in: the Ch'in State or the State of Ch'in (905 B.C.- 206 B.C.), enfeoffed as a dependency of Chough by King Piety of Chough in 905 B.C and enfeoffed as a vassal state by King Peace of Chough in 770 B.C. In the ten years from 230 B.C. to 221 B.C., Ch'in wiped out the other six powers and became the first unified regime of China, i.e. the Ch'in Empire.
* Sui: the Sui dynasty (A.D. 581 – A.D. 619), a transitional period between the Northern and Southern Dynasties period and the great T'ang dynasty. In February, Emperor Calm of Northern Chough abdicated and handed his throne over to Chien Yang, the first emperor of Sui, who reunified China.
* King Strict: King Strict of Chough (904 B.C.- 829 B.C.), the tenth king of Chough, reigning from 879 B.C. to 843 B.C.
* Hai Hu: Hai Hu (230 B.C. or 221 B.C.- 207 B.C.), the second emperor of the Ch'in Empire, reigning from 210 B.C. to 207 B.C.

译 者 简 介

赵彦春教授致力于中华经典典籍的翻译和传播。他持表征之神杖，舞锐利之弧矢，启翻译范式之革命，将诗歌之"不可译"变为"可译"；将"译之所失"变为"译之所得"；将中华五千年的语言、哲学、诗学和美学的智慧融为一体，进行大胆尝试而细腻创新；他坚持译诗如诗，译经如经，从音韵形式、思想内容和文化意蕴上完美诠释了音美、形美和意美的统一；他相信语言与宇宙同构，将翻译的"诗学空间"不断延伸和拓展。

为了讲好"中国故事"，引领中国文化"走出去"，他带领一批志同道合的专业人士兢兢业业，孜孜不倦，锐意进取。从编辑、出版经典译著到举办国学外译研修班，从召开经典外译与国际传播学术研讨会、举办中华文化国际翻译大赛到创办 *Translating China*（《翻译中国》）国际期刊，他和同仁将忙碌的身影融入到了中华文化复兴的背景之中。

他带着"赵彦春国学经典英译系列"等一大批优秀的翻译成果走向世界，向世界展示中华文明的无尽魅力。

他无愧为中华典籍传统文化的传承者和传播者。

About the Translator

Professor Yanchun Chao devotes himself to the translation and transmission of Chinese classics. To inherit the traditional Chinese culture, he holds the divine scepter of Representation and sways the sharpness of bow and arrow to initiate a paradigm revolution out of fallacies, turning "untranslatability" of poetry into "translatability", "losses of translation" into "gains of translation", integrating the wisdom of five thousand years of Chinese language, philosophy, poetics and aesthetics to make bold attempts and exquisite innovations; he insists on translating Poesie into Poesie and Classic into Classic, perfectly interpreting the beauty of sound, form and sense from prosodic features, ideological contents and cultural implications; he also believes that language is isomorphic to the universe and constantly expands the "Poetic Space" of translation.

To tell good "Chinese stories" and lead them to "go global", he guides a group of like-minded specialists to work with diligence and fortitude, editing and publishing classic translations, convening seminars on English translation of Chinese culture, holding conferences on Classic Translation and International Communication, organizing "CC CUP" International Chinese Culture Translation Contest and editing an international journal *Translating China*, their busy figures silhouetted against the background of the revival of traditional Chinese culture.

With "Yanchun Chao's English Translation Series of Chinese Classics" going global, he shows to the world the endless appeal of the Chinese civilization.

He is a true inheritor and promoter of Chinese classics and traditional Chinese culture.